For I Have Sinned

For I Have Sinned

A novel by
Gerard Rose

Carmel, California
April 2013

This book is a work of fiction based on historical fact. You are invited to both enjoy and learn from the story.

For I Have Sinned

For more, please go online to GerardRose.com.

Cover design & photograph by Tony Seton.

Published by SetonPublishing.com.

ISBN-10: 1484048563
ISBN-13: 978-1484048566

Printed in the United States of America

Table of Contents

Publisher's Note

Gerard Rose is simply a fine man who has lived an incredibly rich life and he has written about it. His format is historical fiction, and in both *Bless Me Father*, which came out in August 2012, and now *For I Have Sinned* he demonstrates his considerable skill as a storyteller.

These books are more than a good read; they define a vital time in our nation's history, and illuminate critical aspects of our society. Gerard writes without an agenda, really, except to celebrate nobility and love.

I take considerable pride in having instigated Gerard's decision to publish his first historical novel, *The Early Troubles*, which tells of Ireland rebelling against the British around 1917. Five months later, he had written *The Boy Captain*, a marvelous tale based on the life of Joshua Barney, an American Naval hero of the Revolution and the War of 1812. Both stories were thoroughly researched.

Gerard didn't have to do as much research for *Bless Me Father* and now *For I Have Sinned* because the characters and the events in these books were all very close to home, and as such, are described both poignantly and with power.

Thank goodness, Gerard is not finished writing, for his insight on life provides useful perspective for us all.

Tony Seton
Carmel, California

i

For I Have Sinned

Dedication

This Book Is Dedicated To My Best Friend

For More Than Twenty-Five Years,

Robert J. Koontz

Thanks For Always Being There For Me.

For I Have Sinned

Preface

I know that many of you who read this book will encounter characters whom you recognize as someone you know, or even as yourself. But you are wrong. Everybody you read about in this book is fictitious, purely and simply.

I admit that I have brazenly borrowed and used people's actual names in order to spike sales of my book to friends who love to see their names in print.

The truth is that the only real person in this book is my friend who was killed in Vietnam, Patrick Kelly. And that isn't his real name, since I changed it to protect the privacy of his family.

To those of you who have read *Bless Me Father*, I apologize in advance for what will almost certainly be needless repetition. But I have picked up where I left off in that novel, and I am hopeful that you will find this modest sequel about the life and times of Jay and Lynn Ryan worthy of your time.

And to the real Jay and Lynn Ryan, who have no relationship whatsoever to the main characters in my narrative, I give you my thanks for the use of your names.

Gerard Rose
Carmel, California

For I Have Sinned

Chapter 1

Trouble in Paradise

It was a typical August day in suburban Sutterville, California. The temperature was well over one hundred degrees, and I had just dropped off my son and daughter, Joseph and Maura Ryan, as well as their new nanny, Fiona Ayers, at a movie theater located near Sutterville State College.

I was parked along a shady street nearby the theater, and although my mind was wandering, I was ostensibly reading bits and pieces from a John Grisham novel, and I was drinking lemonade from a thirty-two ounce container I had just purchased at a nearby convenience store.

I figured I had two hours to kill before I would be picking up my children. And after reading for half an hour or so, I thought I might take a walk along the nearby Auburn River

I was sitting in my new Mercedes convertible sedan, a conceit I allowed myself after a two-week jury trial in which I had successfully defended one of my biggest clients, Atlantic Pacific Railroad, in a wrongful death lawsuit.

My fee, which was the largest I had earned since opening the Law Office of Jay Ryan, had been substantial. And, of course, I was pleased and quite proud that I had won.

But I had mixed emotions about my victory.

The plaintiff was an eight-year-old girl whose mother was a

prostitute. The mother and her boyfriend had been crossing my client's tracks in a remote area south of Sutterville, and they were killed when one of my client's locomotives plowed into the side of their automobile at about two o'clock in the morning.

There was no crossing gate where the accident occurred, and the attorney representing the little girl argued quite passionately that the absence of a barricade was the sole cause of the double deaths.

For my part, I argued that the boyfriend who had been driving the car had an unobstructed, starlit view for miles in each direction, and that his blood alcohol level, which was three times the maximum limit fixed by the State Legislature, left no doubt about who was responsible for the terrible accident.

The problem, of course, was that little girl.

She was as sweet and bright as any child I had ever met, very cute, and I knew from formal discovery I had taken in the case that she had no family to take her in.

She was now "temporarily" residing at a foster care facility maintained by the State of California near William Mark Park, and I had been told by her caseworker, who was a woman I had known in grade school, that she was unlikely to be adopted.

According to my friend, the little girl had two strikes against her. First, she was black. And second, she was too old to be taken in by most couples who were in the market for an adoption.

I had briefly entertained the thought of adopting her myself. But in the years since my wife, Jane, had died while giving birth to our son, I had found that raising two children as a single parent was extraordinarily difficult. There was simply no way I could add a third child to my young family without extending myself in a way that would be unfair to both my son and my daughter.

As I mulled these thoughts over in my head, I became vaguely aware that someone was standing next to my car, speaking to me from the sidewalk. He was Hispanic, and appeared to be in his late thirties or early forties. He asked me where I had purchased my soft drink, and I gave him directions to a convenience store that was about a block and a half away.

My thoughts returned to the little orphan, and I wondered silently whether it was morally right for me to feel good about a legal victory that had deprived her of money damages that might otherwise have mitigated the loss of her mother.

As I was considering this, I noticed that someone was now standing on the street next to my door. Surprised, I looked up and saw a pistol, only inches away, pointed directly at my face. The man holding the pistol was the same Hispanic man to whom I had offered directions only a few minutes earlier. And he was shouting at me, demanding that I should give him my keys.

I was confused, at first, and I found myself fixing my eyes on the rifling etched on the inside of the pistol's muzzle.

At some point it finally struck me that I was in grave danger, and I tried to open the car door to get out.

As I did so, another Hispanic male, who couldn't have been more than eighteen or nineteen, appeared on the scene. He jerked my passenger door open, and was scrambling into the passenger side of my car as the older man shouted at me once again, this time demanding that I give him my wallet.

It was then that I did something really stupid. Instead of

giving him my wallet, I told him "no." Actually, I said "Hell no."

Again, he demanded my wallet, and again I foolishly told him "Hell no" again.

I fully expected him to shoot me, and he was probably thinking about doing just that, when the younger man shouted to the older man, who he referred to as "uncle," that my keys were "in the ignition."

Hearing that, the older man lowered his pistol, roughly pulled me out of the car, shoved me aside, jumped into my driver's seat, slammed the door, and the two men – and my new Mercedes – screeched away and headed off down the street at a high rate of speed.

So there I was, standing in the middle of the street, in a strange neighborhood, with a John Grisham book in one hand and what remained of a thirty-two ounce cup of lemonade in the other.

I stood speechless for a minute or two while I tried to comprehend what had just happened.

My first thought was "how am I going to pick up my kids and their nanny?"

My second thought was that I needed to call the police.

My third thought was to question why had I been so stupid as to refuse to give the older man my wallet.

I had no phone with me back then, but there was an apartment complex across the street, so I walked to its office, and asked to use their phone.

The manager was a middle-aged Hispanic woman who spoke no English, but I knew enough Spanish to tell her I had just been robbed at gunpoint. And she was quite helpful in calling the local police station so I could report the car-jacking.

I then called my father, who lived with my mother several miles away in our long-time family home. When I told him what had happened he became quite upset, and he wanted to pick me up right away. But I convinced him to wait until it was time to pick up Fiona and the children, and to meet me after that at the nearby convenience store.

About five minutes later, as I stood silently in the office waiting for a policeman, I heard a loud bang, like the slamming of a door. I couldn't tell what it was, but it appeared to come from a nearby apartment.

Obviously startled, the apartment manager yelled at me, in Spanish to "*¡Acuesten en el suelo.*" She was telling me to lie down on the floor!

My Spanish isn't great, but I got the picture, and dove to the floor. There the manager and I both lay motionless for what seemed like an eternity.

I could hear shouting just outside the office door, and then a loud pop-pop-pop-pop from what sounded like an automatic assault rifle being discharged.

The sound of automatic fire repeated itself two or three times over the next minute or two, and I fully expected someone with a machine gun to come crashing through the office door at any moment.

But then, gratefully, I heard a siren, and it seemed to be coming from the street adjacent to the apartment complex.

I found out later that the siren came from a police car that was responding to my report about the car-jacking of my Mercedes.

I also learned that there was no connection between the theft of my car and the incident outside the office door, which was apparently nothing more than a drug deal that had gone terribly wrong.

The good news was that I was alive and well.

The bad news was that my car was recovered a week later after a high speed police chase in which the pursuing officer slammed his service vehicle into the side of my Mercedes in a "t-bone" maneuver.

In other words, my car was totaled.

*   *   *   *   *

In retrospect, the car-jacking had a salutary, and even life-altering, effect on me.

Aside from the inconvenience of having to appear in court in connection with criminal proceedings against the car-jackers, and having to present the court with a "victim's impact statement," I was forced to confront the reality that Sutterville was no longer the safe, sleepy city of my youth.

I had been raised in Sutterville, and it was there that I had met and married my late wife.

I had shepherded my children through pre-school and early grammar school in that city, and it was there that I was now practicing law, and flourishing professionally as a solo practitioner.

I was surrounded by friends and family, and for as long as I could remember, I had felt a real affinity for this city with two rivers.

But in recent months I had entertained serious doubts about

Sutterville.

On her first day of eighth grade at our local grammar school, my niece Sarah, who lived only a few blocks away from my home, had been confronted by two girls with knives. She hadn't been hurt, but these were girls her own age.

And I couldn't help but notice that graffiti was appearing more and more commonly in Sutterville's commercial district. More importantly, nobody was bothering to remove the "tags" that were placed by gang members who were apparently staking out their turf.

It was undisputed that drive-by shootings were occurring regularly in a poor neighborhood less than a mile from Sacred Heart Church Parish, where my children were enrolled in its grammar school.

There were growing numbers of homeless people, including women and young children, who camped out each night along the tracks owned by the Atlantic Pacific Railroad, just outside the city.

And Sutterville's politicians seemed unwilling or unable to do anything to address the fact that their city was not only deteriorating, but was very close to being out of control.

My father's family has lived on California's Central Coast for four generations, and not surprisingly, I had many friends and relatives living in the small villages that line Monterey Bay.

My favorite of these, by far, is the beach town of Holy Cross.

Holy Cross is a three-hour drive west of Sutterville, and it is it there I would take my children for weekend outings so we could relax along the blue waters of the Pacific.

In fact, shortly after Jane died, I had bought a three-bedroom beach house in southern Holy Cross, near New

Brighton State Beach. I acquired this second home because I wanted to be able to travel to the ocean with Maura and Joseph anytime I wished, and not have to worry about planning or packing food and clothing.

New Brighton is one of those special places that I have always gone to when I needed a break, or had to deal with something taxing, like a death in the family, or had to make an important decision, or simply needed to have some time alone.

I'm not the first member of my family to feel that way.

*   *   *   *   *

I have an old photograph that was given to me by my grandmother, my father's mother, Mary. It's a simple shot of a horse-drawn wagon covered with hay. And it is standing at the entrance to New Brighton. There is a couple in the wagon, and you can see by the expressions on their faces that they are happy and obviously interested in one another. A handwritten note on the back of the photograph indicates that it was taken by a professional photographer in 1912. And, according to my grandmother, the two people sitting in the hay are she and my grandfather – on their first date.

Needless to say, I'm glad the hayride went well.

In any case, and in my mind, the decline of Sutterville as a family-friendly venue, and my love of Holy Cross, eventually spawned thoughts that some day I might move my practice from Sutterville to Holy Cross, and live full time in my beach house near New Brighton.

Certainly one of the events that pushed me in that direction was the car-jacking of my Mercedes.

But the event that finally pushed me over the edge, more than any other, was a decision by my long time secretary and paralegal, Lia, to marry a physician who had once been a client of my first employer, the Grace Law Firm, and move to Oregon.

For years I had depended on Lia for such mundane tasks as typing my legal papers, organizing depositions, scheduling meetings, and the like.

But it was her wisdom, and her patience with me and my affairs, that were her most important assets. And in that respect she was simply indispensable.

Let me give you an example of what I am talking about.

I can recall numerous occasions when I would write vituperative letters to my legal adversaries. They were typically written when I was all fired up about something or other, and drafting them was a good way to get whatever it was that was bothering me off my chest.

Instead of mailing these letters immediately after I wrote them (as I demanded), Lia would always hang on to them overnight, and then bring them to me the following morning – knowing full well that I could and would reconsider what I had written and drastically soften their tone. And in the process, the letters would improve substantially in their effectiveness.

Once Lia was gone, I knew it was time to change my venue.

Which is what I did.

In the Summer of 1990, shortly after my forty-fourth birthday, I moved with my two children to our beach house near New Brighton Beach.

At the time, Maura was nine and was about to enter third grade. Joseph was seven, and was about to enter first grade.

Jane's mother had died the previous winter, and her passing had taken a heavy toll on my children. She had always been soft spoken, taking a back seat to her husband, Clark, but she took her role as "Nana" quite seriously, and she was always there for us when we needed her.

She had also been incredibly generous to us, and particularly to the children, and virtually every Sunday morning she made it a point to transport them to a large toy store in a strip mall in suburban Sutterville.

In fact, that weekly trip with Nana was something that trumped any other function my kids might otherwise wish to attend.

Ironically, Nana had been killed by a drunk driver on a Sunday morning while she was driving to our home to pick up the kids for their weekly outing together.

The fellow who hit her (head on) was returning to his apartment after consuming heroin and marijuana, apparently in celebration of a drug deal. He had also been drinking, and it was clear that his brain was fried.

Fortunately, he was convicted of murdering her. But by some strange quirk of the legal system, the bulk of the prison term imposed upon him was not because he had killed someone, but because the police had found cocaine in his pocket.

His wrap sheet, which was seven pages long, was a sad testament to the kinds of people who were now driving around Sutterville on Sunday mornings.

Oh, and by the way, he was driving a huge, beat-up sports utility vehicle when he ran into Nana's Honda Civic, and he wasn't even injured.

A candidate for Hell if there ever was one.

Chapter 2

Holy Cross

As might be expected, my children were quite upset when I told them that they would have to change schools; not to mention leave all their friends behind. And I knew they would miss the interaction they had with Jane's father, Clark, their grandfather, and Jane's sister, Auntie Peggy. But I felt I was doing the right thing.

In retrospect, moving to Holy Cross was one of the smartest things I ever did.

Holy Cross is a charming village situated on the north end of Monterey Bay. It is surrounded by dense forests of redwoods and Monterey Pines, and its waters are crystal clear and deep blue in color.

Some of the beaches in southern Holy Cross, including those of New Brighton, are bordered by sheer, tall cliffs that are studded with fossils that are many millions of years old. Indeed, those ancient rocks are so plentiful that they were once quarried and used as building materials for mansions built in the city's oldest section – particularly during the Victorian period.

Holy Cross has a municipal wharf that caters to commercial fishermen as well as tourists, and there is an old-fashioned boardwalk, including a casino, which dates back to the eighteen hundreds.

I remember well the excitement and adrenalin that went through me when, as a nine year old, I was deemed tall enough to ride on the boardwalk's roller coaster, a west coast landmark that was built in the 1920's.

According to my grandmother, who ought to know, she was lying on a beach blanket in front of the Holy Cross casino during one of the major aftershocks of the great San Francisco earthquake of 1906, and she recounted seeing the sand alongside the boardwalk undulating as though it were a wave breaking onto the beach.

Politics in Holy Cross has long reflected the lifestyle of the majority of its residents, i.e., liberal, unconventional, and laid back.

For years locals have referred to the village as the "people's republic of Holy Cross," and nobody was surprised a few years back when the village's then mayor, who was a card-carrying communist straight out of the 1950's, was branded by some his opponents as being "too conservative."

Although the village's ethnic mix has long been diverse (which I love), it has never had gangs, or drive-by shootings, or knifings at its public schools; nor even any graffiti.

In short, it was just the kind of place where I wanted to raise my young family, and it was a great place to practice law.

Chapter 3

Settling In

After moving to Holy Cross, my first order of family business was to find an appropriate school for Maura and Joseph.

Not surprisingly, in view of my own background, I enrolled my children at Holy Cross Parish School. The school is a parochial institution that was founded in the 1860's, and had initially been situated on the grounds of one of Father Junipero Serra's historic California missions.

It is staffed with motivated teachers and has a large student body with widely varied social and economic backgrounds. It was the perfect kind of institution for my youngsters.

My first order of law business was to set up an office. And in this I was most fortunate. I found an old office building in central Holy Cross in which several young lawyers, all of whom acted independently, had a space sharing arrangement with one another.

I had about a dozen clients whom I had represented when I was practicing in Sutterville, and most of them had agreed to stay with me after my move. For that reason, I was pretty much off and running from my first days in Holy Cross.

As I began to settle into life in that village, I was surprised and extremely pleased by the way my family was greeted and accepted by our neighbors.

I had met some of them earlier, of course, when my beach house was a second home, but once we moved to Holy Cross as full-timers, there was a lot of attention paid to us.

People dropped off meals and housewarming gifts, and there was a steady stream of well-wishers who did their best to make us feel welcome.

I had a strong sense that I had found a home for life.

* * * * *

I have always been interested in classical music, including opera, and I had invested in season tickets at the San Francisco Opera while I was practicing law in Sutterville. The idea had been to take clients to the opera, and thereby promote my business.

Every month I would be sent two tickets (chairs A and B) in box W (or the "Abraham Lincoln box" as we called it at the time) at the opera house on Van Ness Street; you may remember it from the movie "Pretty Woman."

But when we moved to Holy Cross, I decided that it might make more sense to take either Maura or Joseph to the opera with me instead of clients.

So we started a new tradition.

Each month one of my children would dress up in their best clothes, and we would drive together to the City and eat at a fancy restaurant.

We would then go to the opera, and after the opera was concluded, we would cap the evening with dessert at one of the City's countless coffee shops.

The idea, of course, was to instill an appreciation for classical music in the minds of my children.

But you never know.

I remember taking Maura to the opera one night, and together we saw a production of Wozzeck by Alban Berg. The opera featured violence, nudity, and a score that was partially atonal, and I was sure that Maura hated it. So I asked her at the end of the first act if she understood why some of the opera didn't have melodies.

"I understand, Dad," she said, "When the music sounds weird, it is because the main character is crazy, and it shows you what is going on in his brain."

In other words, she got the point exactly.

Interestingly, years later, both she and her brother told me that they loved classical music, and that they attributed that love to our trips together to San Francisco.

*   *   *   *   *

Both of my children were also interested in soccer.

So I quickly enrolled Maura in a local soccer club that was affiliated with one of Holy Cross's public grammar schools.

But there was a problem finding a team for Joseph. All the league's soccer teams for boys his age had supposedly been filled with applicants who had signed up ahead of him.

I was told that a new team (and a spot for Joseph) was a possibility, but there was a significant catch. They needed a coach, and that coach had to be me.

In addition, every coach had to agree to be a referee for at least one additional game played on the same day the coach's own team had a game.

That didn't seem like such a big deal at the time. After all, I figured, I would be going to all the games and all the practices anyway, so it wouldn't cause me any particular hardship.

But there were difficulties I didn't foresee.

First and foremost, was the fact that I had never actually played soccer myself, and so I hadn't a clue about the rules of the game, much less any special rules that would apply to first grade soccer matches.

I figured I could get help from my fellow parents, but that was when the second shoe dropped. It turned out that my son's team would be made up almost entirely – Joseph being the only exception – of children from the Holy Cross Orphanage, known simply to locals as "The Orphanage," that was located across town.

In other words, there would be no other parents to help me out.

I also learned that most of the boys on my son's team would be driven to and from our games and practices by an old bus owned by The Orphanage. But the bus wasn't big enough to carry the entire team. So I was required to ferry at least half a dozen of the boys back and forth in my own vehicle.

You will recall that I had been involuntarily deprived of my new Mercedes a year earlier.

Well, fortunately I was savvy enough to replace it with a less desirable vehicle – in this case a Volkswagen van. And when the new soccer season began, I felt more like a bus driver than a coach as I transported my van full of young soccer players back and forth to The Orphanage.

Many of the soccer parents I met during my tenure as a coach and referee told me that they considered the boys from The Orphanage to be outliers.

They didn't live in close proximity to the other children, their parents (if they had any) didn't socialize with "normal" soccer parents, and they came from a world that was more reflective of rejection than acceptance.

I saw things differently.

It was my observation that the people who ran The Orphanage were uniformly loving, competent and hard working.

I couldn't dispute the fact that it was difficult to deal with children whose world included spousal and child abuse, parental and sibling drug use, or simple abandonment.

But overall, I thought the boys were wonderful.

In fact, within a short time after the season began, I was actually looking forward to our games.

When I spoke to my boys about soccer – even though I often didn't know what I was talking about – they hung on to my every word. And when I praised them for a successful maneuver on the field, or even a good try, they would beam as though they had accomplished the greatest feat imaginable.

One day, while I was refereeing a soccer match involving two other teams, the mother of one of the boys shouted loudly at one of the boys on the opposing team, complaining that he was being too aggressive.

In fact, he wasn't, but I wanted to shut the parent up since she had been questioning my calls (with some justification, I should add) and had been quite obnoxious since the game had begun.

Not knowing what else to do, I walked over to her handed her one of the yellow cards all the referees had been given at the beginning of the season to subdue players we thought should be warned, or even ejected, for unsportsmanlike conduct.

As I did so, I told her as firmly and formally as I could that she had been "warned."

She protested that I had no right to "card" her, but my ploy worked: she immediately quit her tirade, and for the remainder of the game she was quiet as a mouse.

One of my orphans, in particular, found a special spot in my heart. His name was Timmy Dolan, and he was about the same age as my son, Joseph. But he was several inches shorter than Joseph, and he weighed far less. He always looked unkempt and emaciated, even though the Orphanage always made sure that all their charges, including Timmy, were clean and well fed.

The thing about Timmy was that he loved being on our team more than anything else in the world, and he loved playing soccer.

I remember the first time I praised him from the sideline for scoring a goal. When he heard me call his name, he turned toward me, smiled broadly – obviously oblivious to what lay ahead as he crashed headlong into the frame that surrounded the goal post.

Then there was the time that I was supposed to transport Timmy, along with five or six other boys, back and forth to one of our games.

I had told the boys that we would be playing our toughest opponent that day, and I knew that Timmy, in particular, was excited about the game.

But when I arrived at The Orphanage, Timmy told me he couldn't join us. When I asked him why, he told me that his mother would be visiting him that day.

He was obviously conflicted about this, because he started to cry. So I told him it was important for him to see his mom, and although we would miss him at the game, everything would turn out just fine.

As I did so I noticed that one of The Orphanage trustees, who was standing nearby, rolled her eyes and shook her head after she heard Timmy speak.

Later that day, when I returned to the Orphanage to drop off Timmy's teammates, I was told by the same trustee that Timmy's mother had never shown up.

But there he was, still standing on the front porch of The Orphanage, scouring the parking lot with his eyes, and waiting for someone he hoped would arrive...but never would.

To elaborate on an earlier observation, I'm not sure I believe in a Hell, but if there is one, Timmy's mother needs to go there, at least for a while.

In any case, at the end of the season, I had a party at my house to celebrate our season.

Well, it's a bit of an exaggeration to call it a celebration, since we had lost all of our games except one. And we won that game because our opponent failed to muster enough players to engage us as a team, and suffered a forfeiture.

At the end of the party I gave each of my players an inexpensive trophy I had picked up at a local awards shop.

On a lark, I had each of the boys' names engraved on the trophies, Timmy's included.

When it came time to pass out awards, and I handed Timmy his trophy, he hooted as though I had handed him the greatest gift in the world.

Later, at the end of the party, as I was escorting the boys to The Orphanage bus, Timmy wouldn't cooperate. He grabbed my leg, and told me he wanted to stay. In the end the only way I could get him to leave was to carry him bodily out to the bus.

I should probably mention that Timmy's parents never reclaimed him. And although he was eventually declared a permanent ward of the state, he was never adopted.

But in spite of his challenges, Timmy did quite well for himself.

With the help of tutors, and the loving staff at the Orphanage, he had finished grammar school, high school, and two years of junior college.

With financial help from three anonymous benefactors, including myself, my father-in-law, Clark Grace, and Donny LeBlanc (who you will read about later), Timmy earned a Bachelor's and then a Juris Doctor's degree from my alma mater, Santa Monica University.

He passed the state bar examination on his first try, and he founded a law firm that specializes in handling consumer protection cases. Almost immediately his law firm became quite well known, and it eventually developed a national reputation for its work on behalf of the needy.

I remember beaming with pride when I read in the Holy Cross *Pine Nut,* that he had donated fifty percent of his first legal fee in a class action lawsuit to establish a scholarship that helped fund the higher education of children at The Orphanage who, like himself, never managed to get adopted.

I'd like to add one more story about Timmy.

At some point during his final year of law school he called me at my office, and asked me if I remembered him.

We hadn't spoken in years, but I answered, of course, that I did, although I played down my response because I didn't want to reveal the source of his financial aid.

For the next hour we had a wonderful conversation about our old soccer team and about his remarkable achievements since that time.

He ended our conversation by thanking me for taking an interest in him, and he told me that our soccer season together was one of the pivotal experiences in his life.

He also wanted me to know that the engraved trophy I had given him at the end of our season was his most prized possession, and that he intended to mount it on the wall in his office when he became a lawyer. And that's what he did.

I guess it was a good idea to form a soccer team with kids from The Orphanage.

Chapter 4

Fiona

If Lia was the glue that held everything together in my law practice in Sutterville, my children's full time nanny, Fiona Ayers, was indispensable in holding my young family together after Jane died, and especially after we moved to Holy Cross.

Fiona was eighteen when she first joined us in Sutterville. She had graduated a month earlier from University College, Dublin, in Ireland, where she had earned dual degrees in English and Irish Literature.

But her degrees belied the reality that hers was a poor family that lived very modestly in a small cottage on the grounds of Castle Banny in County Clare in the west of Ireland.

Her father, Robert Ayers, was a grounds-keeper at the Castle, and her mother, Elizabeth, was a seamstress who worked part-time in a small shop in nearby Newmarket-Upon-Fergus.

Fiona had a sister, Mary, and two brothers, Patrick and Sean, all of whom were much older than she.

All of her siblings had emigrated to the United States years earlier, and I had briefly met her oldest brother, Sean, who worked as a bartender at the exclusive Sutterville Club in downtown Sutterville.

Ironically, that was the same restrictive club – WASPS only

– I had refused to join when I was first made a partner at the Grace Law Firm.

But Sean had befriended my father-in-law, Clark Grace, while working there, and when Sean heard from Clark that my wife had died, leaving me alone with two small children, he suggested that I hire his sister as my family's live-in nanny.

Frankly, I was so devastated by Jane's death that I didn't spend much time searching for help.

But thanks to Clark, within a month of my wife's funeral, Fiona was on a plane bound for Sutterville, ready to assume primary responsibility for my new baby, as well as managing the hundreds of tasks required to keep my young family happy, entertained, and well-fed.

Not surprisingly, Clark had greased all the appropriate skids to assure that Fiona could travel legally to the United States, and work as a nanny without fear of trouble from immigration officials.

Specifically, and by some magic I could never fathom, Fiona had been officially declared by the State Department to possess "unique qualifications" not otherwise available in the United States, which meant that she qualified for and was issued a permanent work visa. Remarkably, Clark had managed to arrange all of this in less than a week.

When Fiona first came to live with us, she was little more than a live-in baby sitter and cook, but she quickly became much more than that.

When she was in her early teens, she had worked on and off as a fill-in cook at Castle Banny, and in that capacity she had become quite capable as a chef. The Lord and Lady of the Castle, Colin and Annie Connelly, had excellent taste, and pleasing them was no easy feat. But Fiona had helped kept them happy and content to the point that they had generously offered to pay her tuition and board if she enrolled in a two-year course at a well-known culinary academy in Paris.

Fortunately for me and my family, she had politely refused. Literature, not food, was her real passion.

But food was a close second, and she was a genius who could produce anything the children and I might request.

I remember once, after she had been with us for only a few weeks, I had asked her to prepare us spaghetti and meatballs for dinner. The baby, Joseph, was still drinking formula, of course, but Maura and I both insisted that our pasta be covered with tomato sauce.

Fiona searched our pantry for tomato paste, or even commercial tomato sauce, and found neither. But she did find some catsup, and a single, overripe tomato, and she announced, proudly, that she could make pasta sauce from those two ingredients. And much to my surprise her sauce was delicious.

But it was Fiona's love of my children, not her culinary talents, that transformed the lives of all of us.

Every night before the children fell asleep, she would regale them with tales she had gleaned from English and Irish literature.

Sometimes she would read them stories from a small library she had brought with her from Ireland. Other times she would sing them Irish folk songs. And other times she would recite poems that she had memorized as school girl in County Clare.

Early on I could tell these were important moments in my children's lives, and as they grew older I would sometimes ask for Fiona's permission to sit in on these very special sessions.

I remember the sad day, when my children were both in high school, that Fiona announced that she had fallen in love with a fellow she had met at a local public house.

She beamed broadly as she told me that she and the fellow would soon be married, and that she would be moving in with him that very week.

Truth be told, the idea that she would be leaving us was devastating, but I didn't let on how I felt. To the contrary, and I gave her a big hug, and told her I was happy for her.

In fact, the announcement caused me so much distress that I couldn't concentrate for weeks, and I found myself spending hour after hour walking along the beach at New Brighton.

When the day of her marriage finally arrived, it was I who took the place of her father, who had died the previous winter, and "gave her away." I did so with all the pride I would have felt had she been my own daughter.

Unfortunately, her marriage did not survive the year that followed.

It turned out that her husband, who was a fine young man from all that I could see, decided that he was gay, and he announced to her shortly after their honeymoon that he was not sexually interested in women, including poor Fiona.

Distraught, Fiona sought and was granted an annulment of her marriage by the Catholic Church.

But the annulment process was time-consuming and painful for her. She had to solicit written, sworn "testimony" from friends and family, and had to give a deposition to a Church Tribunal.

She also had to fill out long forms that asked her about matters she felt were private and very personal.

She also had to appear at a formal trial, during which a Church-appointed advocate, who formally opposed her annulment, humiliated her with arguments that suggested that it was Fiona's failings as a wife, and not the sexual preference of her husband, that had doomed her marriage.

Overall, the process was probably cathartic in some respects, but it left Fiona questioning her own good judgment.

It left me furious with the Church for imposing hurdles to an annulment that should have been quick and easy.

Once the annulment process was concluded, I offered to hire her back if she wished to return to our home.

Indeed, the transition would have been simple, since I needed her assistance as much as ever, and I had maintained her room – including her library – exactly as she had left it.

But she never did come back to us.

Jaded by her failed marriage, and racked by self-doubt exacerbated by the Church proceedings, she returned to Ireland.

There she moved back in with her mother, who was still living in the same cottage in which Fiona and her siblings had been raised on the grounds of Castle Banny.

The last time I visited Fiona, which was about a year ago, she was still living in that cottage, and caring for her mother, a life long smoker who by then was suffering from emphysema.

Her mother looked awful, and she couldn't walk more than a few feet without stopping to catch her breath.

But Fiona looked as bright and pretty as she appeared on the first day she first moved into our home, and she was the picture of health.

To nobody's surprise, I again broached the subject of her returning to Holy Cross, and moving into our home. I reminded her that her room was still exactly as it was when she had left us to marry. I also told her that there were many eligible young men living in Holy Cross (some of whom remembered her from her years with my family), and that she might very well meet the man of her dreams.

Indeed, one young fellow, in particular, who seemed very bright, and who was now working as an attorney at Timmy Dolan's law firm, told me that he had met Fiona while she was going through her annulment. According to him, Fiona was the loveliest person he had ever met, and he assured me that he would be very interested in getting together with her if she returned to the United States.

I mentioned this as well, but she politely refused.

According to Fiona, she had a "job to do," and she wouldn't even consider "walking away" from her duty to her mother.

Caring for others was what she did best in life. And it was like a fountain of youth for her.

I guess we should all be so lucky.

I should add that my children have kept in regular contact with Fiona, using the Internet and other social media (that I haven't a clue about), and they routinely trade advice and stories that continue to enrich all of their lives.

Chapter 5

Maura

As difficult as it was for me to lose my wife, Jane, it was much more difficult for my children to be deprived of the support and unconditional love that only a mother can offer.

This is not to minimize the important role that Fiona and Auntie Peggy played in her life.

But the fact was and is that a mother is not like anyone else, and the absence of a mother created substantial challenges for Maura.

I tried as best I could to be a father and a mother to her, but it quickly became obvious that I couldn't and didn't meet all of her needs.

I remember once as Maura was beginning to show the first signs of growing beyond childhood, that I took her down to the lingerie section of Holy Cross's only department store, and I asked one of the clerks there if she would help Maura find "...things that girls her age might want or need."

The clerk, who was a tall black woman in her late twenties, and who looked like a professional model, smiled, gave me a wink, and told me she understood exactly what I wanted, and that I should come back in three hours.

Three hours seemed like a long time, but I took the opportunity to visit New Brighton's beach.

And three hours later I returned to find that the clerk had apparently gotten the job done. Maura and the clerk who had helped her were both all smiles. And I couldn't have been happier – notwithstanding the fact that fifteen hundred dollars had been added to my account at the store.

But Maura now possessed a full complement of items such as underwear and shoes that I couldn't have helped her with to save my soul.

If Timmy Dolan's mother, and the felon who killed Jane, deserve a spot in Hell, then the clerk from the Holy Cross department store who helped me that day with Maura deserves a spot in heaven.

Chapter 6

The Children Grow Up

A few years after Jane died, I met a young woman in Holy Cross who worked as a day trader. I had helped her with some minor legal problems, and it was obvious that we enjoyed our time together. So I asked her out for a drink, and we got along famously.

So well that for the first time, I thought seriously about "dating" someone. But I was nervous about moving on with anyone at that point.

My heart told me that Maura and Joseph would not be happy if I brought another woman into their lives, and for better or worse I decided that it would be in their best interest if I devoted whatever free time I had to being a good parent.

So I distanced myself from the day trader, and she eventually met and married a lawyer friend of mine.

For their part, my children continued to flourish.

Joseph had a very easy way about himself, and was always popular. Like me, he was a bit of a smart aleck, and he ran circles around his teachers at school.

As for Maura, she seemed to have everything going for her. She was pretty, thoughtful, well behaved, and terribly bright.

But because she was bright, she would sometimes be teased by jealous classmates.

On one occasion she was invited to a sleepover party with a group of her sixth grade classmates, and it turned out that the main sport of the evening was to make fun of her.

To her credit, Maura refused to call me and ask me to take her home, and she did her best to withstand the taunts she received that night from girls she had thought were her friends.

When I saw her the next day, I tried to console her by reminding her that she would be a professional one day, and that the girls who had given her a tough time would probably amount to nothing.

Unfortunately, and although my prediction turned out to be accurate, it wasn't much of a consolation for someone who felt the ultimate shame for girls her age: Maura wasn't terribly popular at the time.

But by the time she had reached eighth grade, she had made some real friends, and to her credit, and theirs, she developed relationships with them that she still enjoys as an adult.

*   *   *   *   *

By the time Maura finished high school, her academic success and her easy way with people – which to my great delight was very reminiscent of her mom – made her one of the most popular students in her class.

It was her experience in college that ultimately gave her the tools and experience she needed to flourish as a young woman, and become the wonderful adult and mother she is today.

But first we had to pick a school that would meet her needs.

As to that choice, and much to her chagrin, I pretty much told her that I would make the final choice of a university for her. I wanted Maura to go to a school on the East Coast, and I wanted that school to be run by the Jesuit order of priests; the same order that ran Santa Monica University. I loved the fact that everyone graduating from a Jesuit school with a degree in liberal arts (which was Maura's interest) automatically had "minors" in philosophy and theology, and whatever her choice of religion when she became an adult, I wanted her to be grounded in the Catholic faith that had meant so much to me when I was Maura's age.

After considering the various schools which had accepted her applications, I "recommended" she go to King George University, an institution of higher learning in Washington D.C. that dates back to the 1700's.

After all, I said, "I'm paying for it."

So after much soul-searching, and even some tears, Maura accepted the inevitable. She left Holy Cross, and started a new life as a freshman at King George University.

From day one she loved it.

Chapter 7

The Victim

Unfortunately, one of Maura's first experiences at King George University was one of the darkest of her young life.

On a snowy night during the second month of her freshman year she was on a date with a fellow student who lived off campus. She had attended a party at his townhouse which was located near Foggy Bottom on the banks of the Potomac River in a well-heeled neighborhood of northwest D.C. The boyfriend had apparently had a few beers too many, and had fallen asleep instead of making sure that Maura made it back to campus safely.

Maura was always self-reliant, and she decided to return to campus on her own.

This turned out to be a terrible choice.

As she stood at a bus stop near her date's apartment, a commercial bus stopped to pick her up. The driver explained that his company had a contract with the D.C. Transit Authority to pick up passengers who needed rides during inclement weather, and since the weather was awful, Maura believed him.

Maura boarded the bus, and as soon as she did, the driver closed the bus door...and locked it.

Maura could see that she was the only passenger on the bus, and she began to grow nervous, but the driver was young, and he was wearing a sweatshirt that said D.C. Community College. So she blew off her initial doubts, and she asked him what year he was in. He responded that he was a freshman, and he added that he would take her to King George University "right away."

He drove toward the university for another block or two, but then he turned right, and headed up a hill, away from her destination.

Maura asked him why he was going in the wrong direction, but he refused to answer, and then he smiled at her in what she thought was a very odd manner.

He continued to drive until he reached a decidedly shabby part of D.C., and he pulled into a parking lot. And it was there he forced himself on her, punching her in the torso and face, and ultimately, forcing her to have sex with him.

At first she struggled, but he was very strong. He tightened his grip around her neck, and he told her he was going to kill her if she continued to resist. So she backed off slightly, and was rewarded, ultimately, when he told her he would let her go free.

But he warned her that if she made "a fuss" he would find her and kill her.

She spent the next half hour looking for a cab, but the weather was cold, she was in a high crime area, and there was nothing to be found.

She started crying, and was ultimately picked up by an old African American couple who lived nearby. When she told them what had happened to her they were appalled, and they drove her to nearby King George hospital, where she was treated for her injuries, and given a "rape kit" that was supposed to be turned over to the police, but never was.

She was also interviewed by the Metropolitan Police, and told by them that she would be contacted by a special victims unit sometime in the next twenty-four to thirty-six hours.

I first heard about the attack a few hours after she had returned to the university. I was in New York City on business at the time, so I was able to get to D.C. a few hours after Maura called.

When I first saw her it almost broke my heart. She was bruised all over her torso and arms, and there was still blood on her face where she had been scratched. It almost killed me to see her this way. But she was unbelievably resilient, and she assured me she would be all right.

Needless to say, I was skeptical, and as it turned out, I had good reason to feel that way.

First of all, the promised "special victims unit" never appeared. And there was a delay of almost two weeks before a detective showed up at her dormitory and asked her what had happened.

And there was an additional two-week delay while the police supposedly searched for the perpetrator.

Maura was incensed by the delays, and she set out on her own to find the man who had violated her.

She went to D.C. Community College and demanded to see photographs of the members of its freshman class. But the Office Manager of the College refused, asserting that their students' "privacy" was more important that her need to identify her attacker.

Maura was furious when she heard this, of course, but as she was leaving the college office, one of the secretaries waived a finger at her and indicated that they should meet outside.

Maura got the hint, and within half an hour she had scoured the College's freshman records and had identified her assailant.

His name was Jesse Brown.

She immediately turned his name over to the Metropolitan Police, and then she waited.

Three weeks later, two policemen showed up at her dorm, and gave her a sheet of paper with Jesse Brown's address.

"What is this?" she asked.

"Well, it's his address," they responded, "so you can take care of him."

After they left, Maura called me and asked what this all meant.

"I guess it means that they won't be prosecuting Brown, and that it's up to us to take care of Jesse Brown, vigilante style," I told her.

I did some research, and discovered that Jesse Brown was the son of a well known African American pastor whose church was located in a poor area of D.C. And it was obvious that his father's political connections were strong enough that nothing would be done to bring his son to justice.

I'm not a boy scout (although I once was), but I've spent almost all of my professional life working within the legal system. For that reason, and as much as I might – and did, briefly – fantasize about taking the law into my own hands, especially where, as here, it would be to avenge a terrible injury to my daughter, the notion that I should simply abandon the legal system and take on Ned Brown on my own was out of the question.

So I called in the heavy guns.

As a young lawyer with the Grace Law Firm in Sutterville I had taken on the case of a fledgling Washington politician, Alan Amitin, and I had been successful in defending him from a multi-million dollar civil claim brought against him by the U.S. Attorney.

Alan was now quite prominent on the Washington scene, and it was he whom I called for help.

Fifteen minutes after we spoke, I received a call from the Chief Prosecutor of the Special Crimes unit of the District of Columbia, and was told that Jesse Brown would, in fact, be brought to justice, and that I could be assured that the government would prosecute him "to the fullest extent of the law."

But I had my doubts.

When I met the prosecuting attorney assigned to the case, Bernie Greenfield, I discovered that he had a stammer, much like the defense lawyer in the movie *My Cousin Vinny*. He startled me by telling me that his boss had informed him that this was his last case, and that he had already hired a mover to take his personal things out of the office.

Then there was the Judge, James Wills.

Judge Wills was African American, and he had had a long and distinguished career as a civil rights attorney. And in his courtroom there was a five foot by eight foot black velvet tapestry, featuring the face of Martin Luther King, Jr., on the wall immediately behind his bench.

I couldn't help but wonder if he was the right judge to fairly weigh a criminal complaint against the son of a prominent African American who was accused of rape and aggravated battery.

But my doubts were quickly dispelled.

Judge Wills proved himself not only to be impartial, but wise as well.

During the trial, when Brown took the stand to testify on his own behalf, the judge's clerk had spoken privately to Maura and had asked her, for the sake of her "privacy," if she wanted to view Brown's testimony via a closed circuit camera feed in the Judge's chambers. She refused the offer. She knew he would lie, and she wanted to face him in open court while he did so.

When Brown argued that Maura had "consented" to his attack upon her, the Judge took over his examination and was so withering in his questions that I had no doubt where this was all going.

Which is not to diminish the case put on by Bernie Greenfield. Notwithstanding his speech impediment, his summation at the end of the trial was as compelling as any I have heard in my decades of practice.

At the end of the day, Jesse Brown was convicted of raping my daughter, and the last I heard of him he was still cooling his heals in a prison in nearby Virginia.

A week or so after the trial was over, I wrote a short letter to Bernie Greenfield's boss, and I told him how pleased I was with the way the prosecution had handled my daughter's case.

And, of course, I sent a copy of my letter to my old client, Alan Amitin.

I didn't think my letter was a big deal, and I didn't expect a response.

But two weeks later I received one from the Chief Prosecutor for the District of Columbia. In the letter (which he copied to Alan Amitin) he advised me that he appreciated my remarks, and that he would soon be taking "appropriate" steps to follow up on the Brown verdict with Mr. Greenfield.

A week after that I received a letter from Mr. Greenfield himself in which he told me that his termination had been rescinded, and that he was being promoted to a supervisory position in the major crimes unit of the prosecutor's office.

I guess it sometimes pays to say thank you.

Chapter 8

Maura's College Years

Notwithstanding the trauma of the sexual assault upon her, Maura eventually managed to rise above it all, and get on with her life. I don't believe I would have had her strength, but she was her mother's daughter, and she finished her remaining years of college with remarkable bravery and aplomb.

While the Brown trial was still in progress, she had met a young man from Wisconsin, Matthew Lands.

He was a classmate of Maura's, and they had dated off and on during Maura's freshman year.

By the time they were sophomores they were inseparable. And by the time they graduated, they were talking about marriage.

This was a godsend in several respects.

First of all, it confirmed for Maura what I had told her since she was a little girl – that she was a beautiful person who would easily attract friends, including the "great love" of her life as my mother had promised.

Second, Matt helped give her a sense of how special she really was. Of course, this was no surprise to me. She had worked as a volunteer in a community outreach program throughout her four years at King George University, and had even received a commendation from the White House.

But it was good to know that someone who loved her was giving her the same message.

Third, Matt encouraged her to cultivate a new relationship with me in which we saw each other as adults, as well as father-daughter.

*   *   *   *   *

I remember one day in the Spring of her senior year that I had flown out to D.C. to visit Maura, and incidentally to view the cherry blossoms that are so beautiful at that time of year. As we were walking along the Capital Mall, she suggested that we visit the Vietnam Memorial.

I thought about it briefly, but I had mixed emotions about my service as a Naval Officer in Southeast Asia, and I told her I wanted to skip it.

But she insisted, and we were soon in line, waiting to enter.

The memorial itself consists of a wall that grows from being relatively short in height to quite tall, and then it shrinks back to short again. The wall is engraved with the names of more than fifty-eight thousand men and women who gave their lives for their country. The names are listed chronologically, by the year they died, rather than alphabetically, and this accounts for the changes in the height of the wall--since casualties were initially small, and then grew as time went on, and then declined as the war wound down.

As we waited in line, there was a book at the entrance to the memorial with all the names on the wall listed alphabetically, so that you could easily find the dates of death of anyone you might be interested in.

But there were three teenage girls immediately ahead of us, and for reasons I cannot fathom, they were throwing the book back and forth to each other like it was some sort of prop. And so I never got the chance to look at it, and chart the location of the names of so many of my friends whose lives were lost in that terrible war.

So, as I walked into the memorial, first downhill, then flat, then uphill, I pretty much glazed over the thousands of names engraved there.

Then, somehow, I spotted a name.

I don't know how I differentiated it from the many names that surrounded it, but there it was: Patrick Kelly, Lieutenant, United States Navy.

Readers of *Bless Me Father* will recall that he was my only real friend during my years as a Naval Officer, and that he was killed during the summer of 1969, blown up while drinking coffee in a little shack on the shores of the Mekong River in Vung Tau, Vietnam.

All of a sudden I started to cry.

Maura was too young to remember me crying after her mother died. And so she had no experience seeing me blubbering like a child.

But that is exactly what I did.

Maura was obviously upset, but she was also very comforting, and she hugged me until I finally stopped.

"I've never seen you cry," she said, "and it's very hard to see you in so much pain."

I responded by assuring her that I, too, was unaware that my feelings were so close to the surface.

At the end of that day, Maura and I both learned something

important about one another, and ourselves. I learned (or affirmed) that she had a gift for comforting others. And she learned that I had feelings about the Vietnam War that I had obviously repressed, and that needed to be vented.

We ultimately agreed that it was a good idea to visit the Vietnam Memorial.

Chapter 9

Maura Moves On

After graduating from King George University, with honors, Maura went on to graduate school in Los Angeles, where she earned a Master's Degree in psychology.

In order to help pay for her masters degree, and to earn spending money, she signed up to work in a program that found jobs for people suffering from autism and Down syndrome.

She found this work incredibly rewarding, and I was delighted that she was doing something meaningful for society.

I would like to add that I learned from Maura that one of the companies with the best record for hiring persons with challenges like autism and Down syndrome is a national pizza chain. I can't and won't name the company; but it rhymes with Pizza Gut. Its pizza isn't all that good.

But I don't care.

Anybody who hires physically handicapped people is okay with me. And to this day I buy their pizza, whenever I have the opportunity.

After earning her masters degree, Maura went on to earn her Ph.D. in psychology. And I am proud to say that her first job after graduating was to work as a therapist at a Veteran's Administration Hospital in California, treating soldiers and sailors who suffered from post traumatic stress disorder.

She eventually married Matt, her long-time boyfriend from King George University.

He, too, had earned his Ph.D., and he landed a responsible job with the Environmental Protection Agency.

They produced two wonderful children.

Now, one of the great joys in my life, is spending time with them, sharing stories, and buying them the kinds of toys I would have wanted when I was their age.

My only complaint about Maura and her husband is the fact that they bought a home and settled in Evanston, Illinois, and Evanston is a long way from Holy Cross.

But I try to travel there as often as I can.

In fact, the TSA security staff at the Holy Cross "International" Airport – they apparently have monthly flights to Canada – greets me by my first name whenever they see me. It turns out that it's good to be a frequent flyer.

Chapter 10

Joseph

I suppose it would be normal, and even expected, that someone whose mother dies giving him birth might have a difficult burden to deal with. "What if," obviously, comes to mind, and so I decided early on that I should constantly remind Joseph that his mother's greatest achievement was producing a second child.

Consistent with that decision, Jane's father, Clark, was a doting grandfather, and he made it clear early on that he and my sister-in-law, Auntie Peggy, would always be there for me if I needed them.

This was not a surprise. After all, Jane had told me that she wanted very much to have a son, and she hoped that he would take after the "old man," meaning her father.

As a matter of fact, Joseph was very much like Jane's father. He was as smart as a whip, he was thoughtful and inquisitive, and he had an opinion on absolutely everything.

In the years before she was killed, Jane's mother, Frances, had always encouraged her husband to spend as much time with Joseph as he could. And Clark responded by teaching his grandson how to fish, hunt and play tennis and golf.

I knew in my heart that Joseph would have made a great lawyer, if he were so inclined, but from his earliest years it was clear that he had other aspirations.

For example, he loved nature, and as a little boy he would spend countless hours at a park near our home feeding ducks and fish.

He was also fascinated with mechanical things.

In fact his first word was not "daddy" or "Maura," or even Fiona, as one might have expected, but "vacuum." He loved taking things apart, and I remember laughing to myself when I returned home from work one afternoon, and discovered that an old grandfather clock I kept in my living room had been disassembled by my then five year old son.

"Daddy, I fixed it," he told me.

Fiona simply shook her head with amused dismay.

But Joseph was also interested in spiritual and scientific things.

Once, when I was attending a parents-teacher conference while he was in first grade, his teacher told me that she had observed him one afternoon as he was apparently talking to himself. She had asked him who he was speaking with, and he told her he was having a conversation with "God."

I also recall his sixth grade teacher telling me that one day she had asked him why he was staring into space. He responded that he was trying to figure out what the effect of gravity would be if you were near the Earth's core.

Clearly, this was not a child who was given to frivolous thoughts!

True to their promise, Jane's family – which included several cousins, aunts and uncles – went out of their way to keep both of my children involved in their family activities.

But most of them were living in Sutterville at the time, and after we moved to Holy Cross, they weren't always able to get together with my children as often as they wanted.

As Joseph worked his way through Holy Cross School, he reminded me of myself at that age.

Actually, he was much more charming than I had ever been. And he was very good at manipulating the few nuns and other women who taught at his grammar school.

He used his personality to his advantage as he sailed effortlessly from class to class, usually without having to exert himself by studying.

By the time he was ready to go to high school I recognized that he needed the same sort of boost I got when I went to a seminary, briefly, to study for the priesthood in the early 1960's.

The seminary was bleak, and I hated it, but it was a perfect forum for teaching me how to study. And I did learn to study. And once I did, I was well armed to fulfill whatever dreams I might have for myself.

Joseph had expressed no inclination to study for the priesthood, and I wasn't sure where he would be bound. But wherever that was, I thought he needed to immerse himself in an institution that forced him to exert himself.

I found the perfect place in nearby San Jose, a fairly large city that was then surrounded by fruit orchards about an hour east of Holy Cross.

The school, Santa Monica Preparatory Academy (which everyone called SMPA) was an all-male institution run by the Jesuit order of priests and brothers.

I learned early on that SMPA was tough.

The days of physically manhandling students, (as had been my experience), were pretty much over by this time, but

Joseph told me, more than once, that he was afraid to mess with the Jesuit brothers. They were more than capable of arranging an instructive boxing exhibition as a way of teaching their charges a lesson.

It was also expensive.

But to his credit, Clark Grace picked up the tab for all four year of Joseph's education at SMPA.

By the time Joseph was ready to go to college, he was well on the road to academic excellence.

But there was a problem: mathematics.

Joseph had always managed to pass his math courses when he was in grammar school, but a number of his teachers at SMPA had told me at parent-teacher conferences that he was sometimes unwilling or unable to explain how he reached the answers he turned in to complex math questions.

In fact, one of his teachers told me he would give Joseph a failing mark in senior mathematics unless he could demonstrate precisely, and in writing, each of the steps he had taken in coming up with admittedly correct answers to his examination questions.

There was an intimation – at the very least – that Joseph's answers might have been copied from other students.

Startled, I made an appointment to have Joseph meet with the head of SMPA's math department, a youngish Jesuit priest named Mark Hedberg, and I asked him to help me figure out what was going on.

On the day Joseph met with his department head, the session began with Father Hedberg giving Joseph a complex mathematical equation, and a request that he solve it as quickly and accurately as he could.

Father Hedberg indicated that he would solve the same equation, and he started to do so as Joseph got to work on a piece of paper handed to him at the beginning of their session.

A few minutes later, Joseph handed Father Hedberg the paper he had been working on, with his answer underlined.

Father Hedberg continued working on the same equation, and about five or six minutes later, he, too, came up with an answer. And to his astonishment, his answer was the same as Joseph's.

This happened a second and a third time, and on each occasion Joseph came up with the same answer as Father Hedberg – but in a fraction of the time.

I met with Father Hedberg after his session with Joseph, and asked him for his diagnosis.

"Is there something wrong with Joseph," I asked, "or do you think he is copying answers from other students?"

"What you have, Mr. Ryan, is a prodigy. He simply works these equations out in his head, and his answers are invariably correct."

He told me he would speak with Joseph's math teacher, and he assured me that Joseph would not receive a failing grade.

He also encouraged me to work with Joseph and make a game of taking equations apart, and then writing down answers each step of the way. Needless to say, I spent as much time as I could visiting Joseph and taking him through the steps required to answer complex math equations.

I even hired a tutor to supplement my own efforts.

Gradually, I could see some sort of a light go on in his brain. And by the end of the semester, Joseph demonstrated that he had gotten the message. He called me from school one afternoon and told me that he had earned the highest mark in his class for senior math.

Alleluia.

Chapter 11

My First Holy Cross Client

As indicated above, I was honored and gratified by the fact that when I first moved to Holy Cross, most of my clients from Sutterville continued to use me as their attorney. This made my transition from practicing in a medium-sized city to practicing in a small town much easier than it would have been otherwise.

That being said, I knew it was important that I also develop clients who lived and worked in Holy Cross, and early on I was lucky enough to find several people who wanted me to represent them.

My very first client from Holy Cross was a general contractor named Phil Parentini.

Phil was overweight, he drank heavily, and he had a bad habit of gambling more money than he could actually afford to lose.

But he was bright, he was very funny, he had a good heart, and he was a great golfer.

He was also married to – and estranged from – a woman who was habitually late. He had a son who he was trying to groom into becoming a professional golfer. And he had a circle of friends that I found absolutely fascinating.

But he had a penchant for getting in trouble.

In fact, he was constantly being threatened with lawsuits, and enough people followed through on their threats that I could have devoted my entire practice to trying to fend off the myriad legal claims that vexed him constantly.

Phil's wife had thrown him out of their house when the two of them had broken up, about a year before I had met him. So Phil had moved into a two-bedroom condominium that was being rented by a fellow he had befriended when the two of them were undergraduates at Stanford.

Remember the story of Don Angelo Bellone, the mafia figure I wrote about in my earlier novel, *Bless Me Father*? Don Angelo was the grandfather of Phil's roommate, Michael Bellone.

But unlike his grandfather, Michael was a building contractor, not a Mafioso, and he was obviously not amused when, the first time I met him, I jokingly asked him why he hadn't gone into the family business.

Later, when Phil and I were alone, he told me that questions of that sort were a sore subject with Michael, and that his family ties were something that Michael never discussed, even with Phil.

But as I had learned when I was still quite young, family ties sometimes trump all other considerations.

I had been representing Phil for about six months when he came to see me one day on what he said was a very confidential subject. After exchanging pleasantries, Phil told me that something unusual had happened to his roommate.

According to Phil, one evening, about a week earlier, Michael and Phil were at their condominium, sharing a bottle of red wine, and discussing the recent death of Michael's father.

Not surprisingly, Michael was upset about the loss.

But then he shared a family secret: his father had apparently suffered a fatal heart attack while bedding down the wife of one of his Mafioso "lieutenants." Apparently Michael's mother had returned home unexpectedly, and the confrontation that followed was simply too much for her husband's heart.

Phil and Michael were laughing about this when they heard a heavy pounding on their front door.

Michael answered the door, and he stood there, with the door open, for almost half an hour, speaking softly with someone who Phil could not see, but who was standing on the front porch.

Phil finally spoke up, asking Michael if something was wrong.

There were a few seconds of silence, and then Michel turned to Phil and said: "I have to go."

Phil asked him where he was going, but Michael didn't respond. Instead, he walked out into the night. Moments later Phil heard a car door slam, and then the sound of a vehicle driving off.

The next morning there was an envelope in Phil's mailbox. Inside the envelope there was a check made out to Phil in the amount of twelve thousand dollars. On the check, someone had written "one year's rent".

There was also a note addressed to Phil, telling him that somebody would be by later in the week to pick up Michael's things.

That was the last Phil ever saw, or heard, from his room-mate.

Well, almost.

Two days later, as Phil was about to leave for work, a subcontractor who owed Phil a very large sum of money – a fellow by the name of Jack Kendall – came by the condominium.

When Phil opened the door, the look on Kendall's face was as angry as any he had ever seen. Kendall's left hand was at his side, but his right held a large wad of fifty dollar bills.

Then, without warning, Kendall swore at Phil, and threw the bills at him, striking him in the chest.

The bills had apparently been held together by a rubber band, but the band had broken, and the bills went flying all over the porch.

Phil was speechless, and he could only stare back at Kendall, wondering what would happen next.

After a moment or two, Kendall turned around, swore at Phil a second time, and then he ran down the street and out of the condominium complex.

When he got his bearings, Phil scrambled around his porch, and he eventually managed to retrieve all the cash that had been thrown at him. He then took the cash inside his condominium. And when he counted it up he realized that it totaled, exactly, the full amount he was owed by Kendall.

That evening, while Phil was eating dinner at a local restaurant, a stranger came up to him and asked him if Mr. Kendall had taken care of his debt. Phil answered that he had, and he asked the stranger what had happened. The stranger didn't respond, but smiled and said simply, "Michael says 'Hi.'"

Holy Cross is a small town, and it didn't take Phil long to hear what had motivated Kendall to show up at Phil's condominium. According to a mutual acquaintance, a stranger with a build like a professional wrestler had gone to Kendall's place of work a day earlier, and had demanded to see him. When Kendall appeared, the stranger dragged him into a small bathroom maintained for employees. Once in the bathroom, the stranger then shoved Kendall's head into a toilet, and had "encouraged" him to take care of his debt to Phil.

When Phil learned what had happened, he immediately made an appointment to see me, and he asked for my legal advice about what he should do about it.

As I indicated above, I'm not one to take the law into my own hands, and I'm certainly not going to encourage a client to do so either.

So I told Phil he should contact his former roommate, and ask him, as politely as he could, to let me take care of his debtors in a courtroom, and not elsewhere.

Unfortunately, I never learned whether that conversation ever took place. Shortly after we discussed the Kendall incident, Phil had emergency bypass surgery, and he died on the operating table.

I'm not sure, but it appeared at the time that Phil had some sort of premonition that his surgery might not go as planned.

On the day before he went into the hospital, he came to my office and he paid off my (then overdue) bill for legal services. And at his funeral, I learned from a couple of his friends that he did the same thing with several others to whom he owed money.

Phil didn't pay much attention to religion, but I thought at the time that his "payoffs" might have reflected his belief that there might be someone in the afterlife who would take care of unpaid debts the way that Michael Bellone's guy took care of Mr. Kendall, albeit it in a celestial manner. So Phil was taking care of business, just in case.

As a post-script I should add that Phil's estranged wife made a noisy entrance at his memorial service, and as was her habit, she did so about fifteen minutes into a homily that extolled Phil's many virtues.

I should also add that Jack Kendall was apparently quite relieved to learn that Phil had passed on.

Small wonder, since he probably owed considerable interest on the money he threw at Phil.

Chapter 12

Perry Knight

Because I remained a bachelor for many years after I lost my wife, and because my home in Holy Cross had a relatively large finished basement – with its own separate entrance – I would occasionally make that room available to friends who needed a place to stay.

As time went on, I provided lodging to several close friends who had found themselves ousted from their own homes by angry spouses.

Eventually my basement became known around Holy Cross as the "Bad Boy's Room."

By far the most notorious resident of the bad boy's room was a former rock-'n-roller by the name of Perry Knight. At least that was the stage name he used when he was cranking out would-be hits during the 1960's.

Actually, in 1968 he did find relative success with a forgettable one-hit wonder with a surfing theme.

Perry was a very bright guy, and like me, he was very fond of music.

But unlike me, he had inherited a lot of money from his parents. And in a way that was a shame. Even though true fame had eluded him, he was very talented, and I always thought that he could have made a fortune on his own as a performing artist if had stuck to his guns, instead of relying on his parents' money.

Perry first took up residence in the Bad Boy's Room after he was told to leave his family home by his then wife, Suzanne, a former model who was, in my opinion as a layman (which, of course, is not worth much) as crazy as a loon.

I remember taking my children along with me one night when I went to Perry's home for dinner. This was several months before Perry broke up with Suzanne, and she and his only child, Ellen, were both there with Perry throughout the evening.

At some point Ellen had supposedly committed the mortal sin of complaining about the food her mother was serving, and upon hearing this Suzanne launched into a tirade against the little girl.

This went on for an embarrassing four or five minutes, and it ended with an accusation by Suzanne that Ellen was "satanic."

On our way home, I remember Maura asking me what it meant to be satanic. My response, of course, was to tell her that Mrs. Knight was very sick, and that her little girl was neither satanic nor anything else that was bad – except for the fact that she had a mother who was out of her mind.

Thus, I was not surprised when Perry told me that he and Suzanne had separated, and that he needed to stay in the Bad Boy's Room for a while.

Unhappily, it was during the time Perry was staying with me that I learned something sad (and potentially life threatening) about him.

I have never been a consumer of hard liquor, and over the years whenever anyone gave me a bottle of Scotch or other spirits (usually at Christmas time) it would typically sit around in my pantry for a lengthy period of time – sometimes for years.

On one occasion, after a family birthday party, a friend of mine had given me twenty 1.5 liter bottles of vodka. His family was mostly made up of people who didn't drink, and he asked me if I would do him a favor and take them off his hands.

So I took them home, and not surprisingly, they sat around in my pantry for at least three or four years.

But when Perry came to live with me, the bottles began to disappear.

It turned out that each day he would drink an entire bottle in the period between breakfast and lunch, and he would then "chase" that bottle with several glasses of wine that he would consume with me as we ate dinner together.

At first I attributed Perry's drinking to his estrangement from Suzanne, and I assumed he would get over it when he got over her – which, considering her mental state shouldn't take very long.

But when I discussed Perry with a mutual friend, Hugh Wilson, who is an internist on the staff on Holy Cross Hospital, and who used to play tennis with Perry, he told me that Perry had serious problems.

Not only was he an alcoholic, but his liver was almost completely shot. And in Hugh's opinion, he was going to die, and probably soon.

And, in fact, he did.

But before he died, he was visited by an angel.

Her name was Remy, and she worked as a fitness coach at the Holy Cross Beach and Tennis Club.

Remy knew about Perry's estrangement from his wife, and she took pity on him – as would anyone who knew Suzanne, which Remy did.

She began taking him on long walks, and she encouraged him to quit smoking and to exercise.

She even helped him fend off repeated legal attacks from Suzanne, who tried her best to destroy her former spouse during one of the most acrimonious divorces Holy Cross has ever seen.

Perry eventually cut back on his drinking, and he adopted a healthy diet that caused him to lose weight and feel better than he had in years.

With Remy's encouragement, he returned to his life-long passion, writing and recording music, which was something he hadn't done in decades.

In fact, he managed to turn out some rock-'n-roll that was good enough to attract the serious attention of at least one talent scout for a major recording studio.

With my encouragement, Perry eventually married Remy, and I served as his best man.

For a brief period, before he finally succumbed to liver failure, he was as happy and contented a person as I have ever known.

Thank God, literally, for Remy.

Chapter 13

High Society in Holy Cross

Like many small towns, there is a group of about two or three dozen people in Holy Cross that is at the center of the village's upscale social life. The group consists of physicians, lawyers, accountants, journalists, developers and politicians, many of whom are members of the Holy Cross Beach and Tennis Club, or simply "The Club."

The undisputed leader of that group was and is a hotelier by the name of Donald LeBlanc, or as we call him, Donny.

Donny was raised by a single mom in rural Iowa. His mother, Eloise, was a school teacher who had moved to Holy Cross with Donny and his brother in the early 1950's.

It didn't take long for Donny to develop a reputation as the person to go to if you needed to get things done in that village.

If Donny couldn't do it, he knew someone who could. And it was all done with a smile and a handshake.

By the time Donny was in his thirties, he was worth far more than anybody else in Holy Cross. And he had gained almost all of his wealth through real estate development.

In his words, "I have never seen a piece of real estate that I didn't covet, and I regret every piece of real estate that I have ever sold."

By the time I met him, Donny was in his forties, and he owned five hotels in three different cities, three apartment complexes and countless single family homes that he rented out to his friends.

His personal residence was a large three story Victorian mansion situated on one of Holy Cross's cliff lined beaches. In the back of the mansion was a renovated carriage house in which he kept a dozen or so classic automobiles.

Perry Knight once told me that in his view there are one or two people in everyone's life whose impact is so significant that their names and faces will almost certainly pop into your head in the moments before you die. And that Donny LeBlanc was one of those people.

Certainly Donny LeBlanc is someone you could not ignore, even if you wanted to, but you wouldn't want to.

You may have heard the line attributed by Alice Longworth to her father, Theodore Roosevelt: "At every wedding he wants to be the bride, and at every funeral he wants to be the corpse."

That accurately describes Donny.

He is loud but not rude, endlessly effervescent, and he immediately fills any room he enters with friendly greetings and his expansive good humor.

He and Perry Knight's father were and are the co-owners of Holy Cross's finest hotel, the Holy Grail, and the combination of Donny LeBlanc and Perry Knight at any social gathering virtually assures that the event will be memorable and fun.

Donny is outrageously formal in his daily attire. In fact, he used to brag that it is impossible to overdress. And he is outlandish in his insistence that whatever he eats or drinks is the best there is.

He is so likeable, and his personality is so infectious, that you could almost forgive him if you took him out to lunch and he ordered the most expensive thing on the menu.

He is generous as well.

I have already recounted his generous – and anonymous – financial contribution to the higher education of young Timmy Dolan, someone Donny had never even met.

It turns out that helping folks in need is a basic part of Donny's DNA.

I happened to learn, quite by accident, that a mutual friend of ours, a commercial real estate broker who was engaged in a bitter custody battle with his ex-wife, and who had been fired from the company he had founded, was drinking heavily and was in deep financial trouble. Without fanfare, Donny put him up at the Holy Grail and found him a new job.

He also arranged an "intervention" by the man's friends and a few family members that eventually led to his becoming clean and sober as a member of Alcoholics Anonymous.

It was widely known that whenever a charity needed a place to hold a fundraiser, it was always Donny who stepped up to the plate and hosted it, whether at his Victorian mansion or at the Holy Grail, and he would invariably pay for drinks and food as well.

The biggest problem in Donny's life was his wife, Borgia.

Borgia was quite pretty, and she was always the life of any party she attended. But she had a flaw: she couldn't stand her husband, and she took every opportunity to let anyone and everyone know exactly how she felt about him.

Once, while our families were on a ski trip together, Maura came to me and asked me why Mrs. LeBlanc always said such nasty things about her husband. Frankly, I had no answer to that.

Eventually, Donny and Borgia got a divorce, and it was messy. It went to trial, unfortunately, and people would go to court each day to watch the spectacle as though it were a sporting event.

Sadly, every unhappy detail of Donny's marriage was bandied about – including blatantly false stories of infidelity and heavy drinking on Donny's part – and these details were repeated around the village by gossips at the Holy Cross Beach and Tennis Club.

Finally, when the divorce was concluded, and Donny was officially single, he was a beaten man.

But the pain wasn't over. Shortly after the trial, his mother died suddenly.

I can't attribute her passing to the publicity surrounding Donny's divorce proceedings, but he had told me while it was in progress that it was taking a heavy toll on Eloise.

Donny arranged a memorial service in his mother's honor. It was conducted at the largest facility available for such affairs: the auditorium at Holy Cross School (to which Donny had been a major donor). And he asked me to give one of the two eulogies that were planned in honor of his mother.

I knew Donny's mother quite well, and I told him that I would be happy to do so. But I was scheduled to be in Court in San Francisco on the same day as his mother's funeral.

He told me not to worry.

On the date of the service he sent one of his private planes up to The City (San Francisco) to pick me up and bring me back to Holy Cross, just in time to offer some observations about his mother.

This is how I ended my eulogy: "So what can you say about a woman who swore like a sailor, drank like a fish, told outrageously bawdy jokes, and constantly hit on younger men, including me? That she was lovely."

And so she was.

Chapter 14

The Holy Grail

It was at the Holy Grail, in its venerable Coop Room, that friends of Donny would gather on special occasions to watch sporting events, listen to political speeches, or simply roast one another at events celebrating life in Holy Cross.

Every Wednesday evening there were live performances on the hotel's grand piano, with everyone singing along to old standards.

The people who regularly attended these special events were called the Coop Group. It was with these people, all of whom accepted me as one of them from the day I moved to Holy Cross, and who were incredibly supportive whenever I needed assistance, that I felt most comfortable...as my children moved from grammar school to high school, and as I grew from being relatively young to middle aged.

Notwithstanding the outrageous political views of many of its citizens, Holy Cross was pretty much divided into two camps.

But unlike most other places, the distinction between the two camps was not between Republicans and Democrats, or Liberals and Conservatives, but whether your sympathies were aligned with the Coop Group, or with its rival and nemesis, the Holy Cross Resident's Association, or HCRA.

The HCRA was headed by three people: a former mayor,

Ken Black; a former village council member, Barbara Amundson; and a so-called "environmentalist," Barbara Stock. As a group, the Coop Group liked to refer to them as Ken and the two Barbie's. Together, and in their minds, these three were the self-appointed guardians of the history and traditions of Holy Cross. And when they spoke, unfortunately, many local residents listened.

In fact, the *de facto* mission of the HCRA was to oppose change of any kind within the village, and to oppose "new" ideas like permitting live music, wine tasting, and Christmas Lights in the village's commercial district.

Ken Black, Barbara Amundson and Barbara Stock were the HCRA's vanguard in opposing all of that.

In his years as mayor, Ken Black had been a popular figure. In fact, he had been re-elected without opposition on at least three occasions. But he was impossible to predict.

For example, he once suggested to Donny LeBlanc that he paint the lettering on the old wooden sign at the front of his hotel, the Holy Grail, in gold leaf instead of white paint. But when Donny appeared before the Village Council to make that change, Ken opposed it.

As another example, Ken once commended the owner of a local coffee house for serving sandwiches during lunch time. But later, when the question of selling sandwiches in coffee shops came before the Village Council, Ken supported a decision by the village Planning Commission that had concluded that such sales were incompatible with the use permit for coffee shops.

Barbara Amundson wasn't much better.

Once when she was sitting as a member of the Village Council, there was an appeal filed by a resident who wanted to cut down a dead tree that was threatening to fall down and crush his house. Barbara was opposed to cutting down trees, dead or alive, for any reason, and she said so to the incredulous homeowner.

When he pointed out that his eight-year old's bedroom was immediately under one of the largest branches of the tree, and his eyes welled up with tears, Barbara leaned over a fellow member of the Council and remarked loud enough to be heard throughout the Council chamber: "I'm sick and tired of hearing sob stories like this."

And on the occasion of an application to the Village Council to allow a tavern owner to have live music in his establishment, her response was to read lengthy prepared remarks – so much for keeping an open mind - which predicted dire consequences for the village. And she concluded with the prediction that the next thing we knew Holly Cross would have "honky tonks."

But in my opinion the worst of the HCRA, by far, was represented by Barbara Stock.

Nobody had ever elected her to anything, but she had assumed the mantle of protector of Holy Cross's older buildings – no matter how decrepit.

Once, when a local developer requested a permit to raze a building he owned, she had filed a lawsuit against him in the names of the "Friends of Holy Cross." According to her lawsuit, the building was "historic and irreplaceable" even though it was only seventy five years old, and had been "red-tagged" by the village Building Department because it was so filled with mold and dry rot that it posed a danger to the neighborhood in which it was located.

On another occasion, she filed a lawsuit which would have required the village to collect and recycle all rainwater that fell over the village so, she insisted, that it wouldn't flow into the "fragile eco-system" of Monterey Bay. This would have mandated the village to accomplish something that was literally impossible, and before it was eventually struck down by the Court of Appeals, it cost the village millions of dollars that could have been better spent on legitimate public works.

Each month the HCRA would host a get-together at the Holy Cross Women's Club during which members would take turns criticizing policies espoused by the Coop Group.

And each year the HCRA would select one of its members to be Holy Cross's Citizen of the Year.

Since the HCRA didn't have all that many members, it was clear to nearly everyone that each of its members had been selected Citizen of the Year at least half a dozen times.

The antics of the HCRA came to a ridiculous head several years before I became a full time resident of Holy Cross. The village was holding an election for an open seat on its Council, and a member of the Coop Group, my friend Paula Croatia, whose father had been a long-time plumbing contractor within the village, was running for that position.

In the middle of the campaign, one of Paula's supporters had committed the unpardonable sin of putting up a lawn sign that supported Paula. The supporter owned a printing business, and not surprisingly, the lawn sign looked quite professional.

But that was the rub.

According to the HCRA, "quaint" signs were good, but "professional" signs were bad, and not in keeping with our village's "character."

Paula was denounced by the HCRA in angry letters to the editor of our village's weekly newspaper, *The Pine Nut*.

Paula's love of Holy Cross was seriously questioned, and even raised as an issue at a candidate's forum held by the Holy Cross Business Alliance.

Paula was outraged, of course, and she enlisted the help of Donny and the Coop Group. Together they raised nearly Five Thousand Dollars, and they bought ads on radio (gasp) and television (oh my God) that questioned the thesis that lawn signs were somehow the harbinger of our village's destruction.

Not surprisingly, the HCRA countered with a whispering campaign, the gist of which was to accuse "big money interests" of taking over the village.

But in the end, the Coop Group had the final word.

Paula was elected to the Council by a huge majority, and for a while, at least, the HCRA was pretty much relegated to awarding its members the title of Citizen of the Year, year after year after year.

Paula went on to become one of the most successful and thoughtful Council members our village has ever produced.

She had a gift for making decisions that made sense. Indeed, whenever she and I differed on a matter in controversy, I had to do a second analysis to see if I had missed something.

But her finest quality was her good heart.

She couldn't walk down the street without stopping to speak to people she knew, which included almost everyone, and in that respect she was very much like her father: someone you liked, respected, and could rely on to do the right thing.

She was primarily responsible for updating the village's General Plan, for establishing the village's first multi-year budgets, and for bringing live television coverage into Village Council meetings.

These actions, and actions like them, were all loudly denounced by the HCRA.

But fortunately, nobody listened...at least for a while.

Chapter 15

Home Alone

When it was time for Joseph to go to college, I strongly encouraged him to go to King George University, as did his sister, who was about to start her junior year at that institution.

I thought that Maura could use the companionship, and since she and Joseph were always close, I was hopeful they would keep an eye out for one another.

In fact, as it turned out, the decision was a good call for all concerned.

For her part, Maura loved having her baby brother around. She would counsel him on girlfriends, classes/teachers, and people and places to avoid. And at least once a month she would take her brother out for drinks at Trattoria Il Formagio in nearby Chevy Chase, Maryland.

For his part, Joseph loved being shown the ropes by his sister, and he was particularly happy when she would set him up with girls she had deemed worthy of her brother's attention.

For the next two years, Maura and Joseph were as close as they had ever been. Indeed, they both told me that neither of them had ever been happier.

The bad part about Joseph going to school on the east coast was that I was now alone in California. Even when he was boarding away in nearby San Jose, I always felt that he was close by. Now it would take a long plane ride to visit my children, and it was a loss that I felt acutely.

After thinking it over, I came to the conclusion that I must accept the fact that my children were out of the nest, and that I needed to focus on the rest of my life.

The matter of my future came up one spring night when my children and I we were having dinner at Trattoria Il Formagio. I had flown to D.C. on business, and, of course, I wouldn't pass up an opportunity to visit Maura and Joseph.

At some point during the meal I asked Maura what she would do after graduation, which was fast approaching. She had told me for years that she wanted to be a clinical psychologist, and she confirmed that was still her goal.

When I told her that I approved, and that I was proud that she had chosen a profession that called for service, she asked me what I planned to do when she and Joseph started having families of their own.

I paused for a second, and told her that I might begin volunteering for Holy Cross's legal aid organization. But frankly, I hadn't really given any serious thought to actually doing what I had always encouraged them to do, that is, to serve.

This was something that had tugged at my conscience since I was quite young. In fact, that had been my primary motive for attending a minor seminary and studying for the Catholic priesthood when I was a sophomore in high school.

While I was there I learned quickly that the priesthood was not for me, but the need for service, and the idea that I had to do something for people in need, came back to me again and again.

I remember when I was a Naval Officer in Viet Nam that a friend of mine, who was serving there as a gunnery officer on a destroyer escort, told me that he had saved an entire village from destruction. His ship's executive officer had given him an order to shell the village, but my friend knew that the "exec" who gave him the order was not acting rationally, and was, in fact, acting on his own. So he refused the order. The exec became furious, of course, and he ordered my friend to be placed "in hack," i.e. confined to his quarters. But my friend's courage in standing up for the right thing made the exec fearful of ordering anyone else to open fire, and the village was spared. I thought at the time that I would have given anything to have had such an opportunity.

As it happened, the challenges calling for such service that I faced in Southeast Asia were far more mundane than those of my friend.

*   *   *   *   *

Every so often an opportunity for service does come along.

Once, shortly after I moved my practice to Holy Cross, I remember being approached by two sisters, both widows, who asked me if I could help them with a real estate problem.

After speaking to them for a few minutes it became clear that a fast talking "developer" from the San Francisco Bay area had taken all of their savings, and had done so under the guise of building a "spec" house as an investment in rural Oakland.

I made a few calls, and quickly came to the conclusion that

the spec house didn't exist, and that the sisters had been swindled.

I'm not the most eloquent lawyer on the planet, but I do have a gift when it comes to demand letters. And when I'm not restrained by Lia – she let the reins go on such occasions – my letters can be truly frightening.

So as the two sisters waited, I drafted one of the meanest, nastiest, threatening letters I have ever produced, and sent it via overnight mail to the developer at his office in San Francisco.

The gist of the letter was my demand that he deliver me a cashier's check for the full amount of the sisters' investments, and that he have it in my hands no later than by 4:00 p.m. the next day, or all sorts of terrible things would happen to him.

Sure enough, at approximately five minutes before 4:00 p.m. the next day, the developer himself arrived at my office, huffing and puffing.

He was actually sobbing, and he asked my receptionist to forgive him as he handed her a cashier's check for the full amount I had demanded.

As he left my office building, and was walking out to his car (which he had left running), the two sisters came out of my office library, where they had been waiting to see what happened.

Needless to say, they were incredulous that they had actually recovered their savings.

Then they did it.

They asked me how they could repay me for the service I had provided them.

I must say that for my entire professional life I had waited for an opportunity to give the response that I gave them that afternoon: that the smile on their faces was payment enough for me.

It truly was.

Unfortunately, opportunities like that are rare in the kind of law that I practice.

But it did happen, at least that once.

Chapter 16

Politics

It wasn't very long after my conversation about service with my children at Trattoria Il Formagio that an opportunity to serve came to me in a totally unexpected way.

Patty Gambino, a member of the Holy Cross Village Council – and a friend of both Paula Croatia and Donny LeBlanc – had run across me in downtown Holy Cross and asked me if I would join her for lunch. I suggested we meet at the Coop Room, but she demurred and suggested we meet at a place that was more private.

We ended up meeting at a coffee shop located near the interstate about five miles outside Holy Cross. But our quest for privacy turned out to be for naught. Patty and I together knew virtually everyone in the restaurant.

I guess that's what it means to live in a small town.

In any event, Patty told me that she had wanted privacy so we could discuss a new opening on the Holy Cross Village Council. Specifically, she wanted to know if I would be willing to run for one of two seats that would be filled by an election that would be held in April of 2000, which was about four and a half months away.

I had never considered running for public office, and I was surprised by her suggestion. In fact, at the time I had a pretty low opinion of most politicians, Patty and Paula excepted.

I remember once responding to a request by Donny LeBlanc for a campaign contribution by saying that you shouldn't give money or attention to politicians because, in the words of a friend, "...it only encourages them."

But before I knew it, it was I who was the would-be politician, and it was I who was asking folks for money to support my first political campaign.

*　　　*　　　*　　　*　　　*

There are several things most people don't know about political campaigns and the politicians who run them.

First and foremost is the fact that it takes a lot of work to get yourself up to speed on the issues that matter for a given public office.

In Holy Cross, the biggest issues facing the Village Council related to the protection of the ocean and beaches that make up the southern and western borders of the village, and the challenges posed by development on the village's meager resources.

In order to become conversant on those and other relevant issues I had to spend countless hours with Paula, Patty, and several of their friends who sat with me and patiently fed me the kinds of questions I could expect to hear during the campaign.

I learned that you would be expected to attend candidate forums, service club meetings, and all-important "coffees." They weren't really coffees, but rather informal gatherings at someone's home where eight to ten people who would sip wine and nibble cheese and crackers while listening to presentations by a would-be office holder.

Candidates were also expected to walk through various neighborhoods, and offer their views to people who happened to answer the door; many of whom would consider the campaigner a pest, at the very least, for interrupting their day.

Second, it takes a lot of money to conduct a political campaign.

This is actually a multi-step process.

You begin by registering as a candidate, both with the village and with the state, and you round up the signatures of a minimum of one hundred voters who attest on a village petition that they support your candidacy.

You then establish a bank account to house political contributions, you select a treasurer and a campaign manager, and you buy campaign buttons and similar "swag," all in the hope that the local electorate will take you seriously.

Then you advertise for, and host, an all-important campaign kick-off party, and you hope to God that somebody actually shows up.

In my case, the registration and signature processes went fairly smoothly. I had taken my petition to a Coop Group luncheon that happened to coincide with the announcement of my candidacy, and I obtained most of the signatures I needed at that single event.

I had also enlisted my best friend and fellow lawyer, Robert Koontz, to function as my treasurer.

And in a major coup, I had persuaded a former Council candidate, Frank Perry, to serve as my campaign manager. Frank was an ex-cop, and he had never been elected to political office, but he was smart, savvy, and he seemed to know everyone in the village.

Finally, I was extremely fortunate when almost two hundred people showed up at my kickoff party, which, of course, was held at the Holy Grail.

Surprisingly, many of these people each contributed a whopping ninety-nine dollars, the maximum an individual can legally contribute to a candidate without having their name, address, employer and other information, reported to the state's Fair Political Practices Commission.

Even more surprisingly, there were two contributions in excess of $1,000 each from two donors, one of whom, as you might have guessed, was Donny LeBlanc.

To my amazement, by the end of the evening my campaign coffers were swelling with more than eight thousand dollars.

It takes hours and hours of campaigning to gather the votes necessary to win an election.

Sometimes this happens informally, as when you run into voters who stop you on the street and ask you about your position on a particular issue. And sometimes the editorial staffs of local newspapers will ask you to come by and answer questions.

This activity becomes quite heated during the final two weeks of the campaign when the candidates stand in front of the Holy Cross Post Office from 11:00 a.m. to 1:00 p.m. and hand out their final position papers. They do so knowing that most of the people they are importuning have already cast absentee ballots, and even if they haven't, they have undoubtedly decided who they will vote for, and simply wish they could be left alone.

All of this comes to a crescendo on election night when the candidates and their most ardent supporters gather for an official counting of the ballots at the Holy Cross village Hall, consuming punch and cookies.

I went through each grueling step of this arduous process, and although I cannot say that I enjoyed campaigning, it did teach me a lot about people, and even more about myself.

At the end of the process, we all gathered together at the Village Hall. I stood at the front of the Hall with Patty Gambino, Paula Croatia, Frank Perry and Bob Koontz.

My two opponents, both of whom were newcomers to the political process, were also at the Hall, and together we traded jokes and other pleasantries as we waited for about two hours as votes were counted by the County Registrar of Voters.

There were two open seats on the village Council, and when the votes were finally counted, I came in third, behind the second place candidate by fifteen votes.

In other words, I lost.

I can't pretend that I was happy about the results.

When the editor of the Holy Cross *Pine Nut* asked me for my reaction, I congratulated the winners, and I quoted Abraham Lincoln's famous comment after he was defeated in a multi-party race for a seat in the Illinois State Legislature: "It hurts too much to laugh, and I'm too old to cry."

Upon reflection, I could tell myself that I was grateful that I had garnered as much support as I did. I was consoled by one of my favorite lines from the most quotable American ever, Theodore Roosevelt: "Far better it is to dare mighty things, to win glorious triumphs, even though checkered by failure, than to take rank with those poor spirits who neither enjoy much nor suffer much, because they live in the gray twilight that knows neither victory nor defeat."

As it turned out, there was a consolation prize in the election.

In the same vote in which I was defeated, another member of the Village Council, my friend Patty Gambino, was elected Mayor of Holy Cross, thus opening up her seat on the village Council for the remaining two years of her term.

On her first day as Mayor, Patty nominated me to fill her old seat, and Paula Croatia seconded the nomination. On that same day a unanimous Village Council voted to make me one of its members.

Thus began what eventually became a six-year stint as a Village Council member.

Chapter 17

Political Office

In all fairness, and I've been as guilty of this as anyone, it is easy to criticize politicians.

But I think that most people who do so haven't a clue about the time and effort our elected officials put into jobs that offer little or no financial remuneration – much less the gratitude of the public – and whose primary reward is knowing they helped make life a little better for their fellow citizens.

In that regard, the critics are simply wrong.

Again, let me offer you an observation from Theodore Roosevelt: "It is not the critic who counts: not the man who points out how the strong man stumbles or where the doer of deeds could have done better. The credit belongs to the man who is actually in the arena, whose face is marred by dust and sweat and blood, who strives valiantly, who errs and comes up short again and again, because there is no effort without error or shortcoming, but who knows the great enthusiasms, the great devotions, who spends himself for a worthy cause; who, at the best, knows, in the end, the triumph of high achievement..."

I can't pretend that the office I held was anything like that contemplated by President Roosevelt, but I think it is fair to say that the vast majority of holders of public office have earned our thanks.

Looking back on my six years as a minor politician, there were four things I learned about public service as a Council member.

The first thing I learned was that you have to read literally hundreds of pages to prepare for a typical Council meeting. And since many of the matters you will be considering are complex, you can't speed through your packet.

Normally it takes three to four hours to fairly take in all the things you need to know to avoid looking like an idiot.

The second thing I learned was that you have to be endlessly patient when the public addresses you during Council meetings. Invariably, a few of them – referred to by veteran council members as the "usual subjects" – will go on endlessly, and sometimes mindlessly, to the point that you want to scream.

On the other hand, and in all fairness, most people are unused to public speaking, and they are quite nervous when they address the Council. And in most cases, their input is quite helpful in sorting out the "right" decision on a given issue.

The third thing I learned was that time preparing for and attending Council meetings is just the tip of the iceberg you encounter when you represent the people.

It turns out that each Council Member is also assigned collateral duties on other public bodies, and the time you spend on those duties can dwarf the time you spend on matters strictly related to Council meetings.

In my case I was assigned to the public body which oversees the redevelopment of what was once a military outpost just south of Holy Cross on Monterey Bay. I was also assigned to the board of the Village Authority which runs the Holy Cross ambulance service.

And the fourth thing I learned was that anyone who goes into public life with the expectation that they will be loved, or even appreciated, by their constituents is going to be disappointed.

The reality is that any vote you cast on a controversial subject – that is, anything that doesn't promote babies or puppies – will irritate some, and occasionally many, of your fellow residents.

In my case, it was not unusual to see myself pilloried in diatribes published in newspapers, newsletters, and web sites that served the residents of Holy Cross.

I often felt that the only thing that was missing was villagers storming the Village Hall with torches and pitch-forks.

Even that wouldn't have surprised me.

But you have to be thick skinned if you want to survive in politics, and as I spent more and more time on the Village Council, I got to the point that criticism meant almost nothing to me.

I'm not sure that is a good thing. But it's the reality of public service.

Chapter 18

My Second Race for Public Office

After losing in my first attempt at elective office, my ego was bruised and I was discouraged. I had put on the best campaign that I could muster, and yet I had obviously failed to catch the imagination of the public.

In the end, I had been appointed to my Village Council to finish out the last two years of Patty Gambino's term on the Council.

At the end of those two years, I had to decide whether I was going to run for a four year term of my own.

I talked it over with Patty and Paula Croatia, and we decided we would all run again, though not as a slate. Everyone knew that "slates" were anathema in Holy Cross, and even though everybody knew we were cooperating with one another, we had to make it appear that we were disconnected.

We were expecting a vigorous campaign, but we were shocked when we saw who took the field against us.

Three members of the HCRA, including former Mayor Ken Black, former village Council Member Barbara Amundson, and self-proclaimed environmentalist Barbara Stock, announced that they were running as a slate.

The smart money said they would crush us.

But on the day they kicked off their campaign, they did something that was completely out of character. Not only did they underscore the fact that they were running as a slate, but they passed out cheesy looking t-shirts and, so help me God, lawn signs.

What had prompted this HCRA "dream team" to break three of the most time-honored (albeit unwritten) rules of Holy Cross politics was anybody's guess, and I guess I will never know what they had in mind.

But as the campaign went on, Patty, Paula and I all had a growing sense that momentum was beginning to move to our side.

When the Holy Cross *Pine Nut* held a candidates' forum, the audience seemed overwhelmingly supportive for Patty, Paula and me.

On election night, as we met at the village Hall to watch the votes being counted, I was delighted, but not surprised, when the City Clerk announced that we had beaten the HCRA slate in a landslide.

Chapter 19

My Last Campaign

Four years later, after having served six years in office, I felt I had accomplished many, if not most, of the goals I had set for my time on the Council.

I was very proud of a pathway I had promoted along a busy street to protect the safety of people walking down to the ocean.

I had also championed a ban on smoking on our beach.

My somewhat shameless slogan had been, "Keep your butts off our beach." and it worked. So by the time I left office, the amount of trash that had to be removed from the beach each week had dropped precipitously.

But my proudest achievement related to my job as the President and Director of the Holy Cross Fire/Ambulance Authority (the HCFAA), an entity which provided ambulance service to Holy Cross, obviously, and which was virtually unknown to the voters of my city.

I had assumed the Directorship of that entity solely because of my position on the Village Council, and at first I hadn't given much thought to its mission.

But the more I learned about the Authority, the more I became interested in its success.

The alternative to the HCFAA was the county's contract

ambulance provider, California Pacific Ambulance Service ("CPAS"), an entity which promised to deliver ambulance response to its constituents within twelve minutes of a "911" call.

I studied the paperwork for the HCFAA, and discovered that on average it was responding to emergency calls within eight minutes of a 911 call--which was far better than CPAS's response times; they generally complied with their contract requirements.

That seemed good, but after doing further research I decided that even eight minutes was too long, and that lives could be saved if we could shave our response times down to seven or even six minutes.

I instituted a policy that would require our ambulance responders to personally appear at our monthly Board meetings and discuss, in detail, each and every response time which exceeded eight minutes.

Not surprisingly, the employees didn't like attending Board meetings, and they resented having to explain delays in their response times.

Then something amazing happened.

Over the next twenty-four months our response times fell below eight minutes, and then below six minutes, and then below five minutes.

By the time I left the Council, our response times had dropped to an incredible average of two minutes.

I wish I could take credit for this accomplishment, but the credit duly went to my rank-and-file employees, who eventually took it as a matter of pride that they could beat the county's provider by reaching the victims of heart attacks and other maladies by as much as ten minutes faster than their competitor. And in the real world, this meant saving lives.

About a month before I left office, I attended a Village Council meeting at which we gave a citation to one of our ambulance employees. He had saved the life of a patient who had suffered a myocardial infarction by reaching his home two and a half minutes after his wife had called 911, and by restoring his breathing by giving him CPR.

The patient was a physician and a friend (not to mention a regular at the Coop Room), and he told the Council that it was his professional opinion that he would have died if his treatment had started twelve or even ten minutes after his wife's call to 911.

For me, saving even a single life was worth the hours I had to spend dealing with fire/ambulance issues.

Unfortunately, most citizens of Holy Cross had no idea what had been accomplished in their name by their Village Council.

Midway through my sixth year on the Council, the HCRA found a candidate who gave them an opportunity to wrest control of the Council away from members of the Coop Group, i.e., Mayor Patty Gambino, Council member Paula Croatia, and myself.

The HCRA candidate, Rolly Richards, was the grandson of the man who had invented a computer chip that had revolutionized the Internet. He was young, he was handsome, and he was incredibly wealthy. But most important, he was ambitious, and he used the SCRA as his base to achieve higher office.

He allied himself with two other candidates, including a former member of the Coop Group, and he promoted himself and his two allies as a slate that was an "environmental alternative" to Patty, Paula and me.

Richards kicked off his campaign by hiring a focus group from the state capital to make telephone calls to Holy Cross residents in which the residents were asked if they were happy with the anti-environmentalist policies of the current Village Council.

I had always seen myself as someone who was sensitive to environmental issues, and I knew that Richards' campaign was grounded on a lie.

But as in war, one of the first victims of a political campaign is the truth.

When Richards began pouring tens of thousand of dollars behind his slate – a figure that was ten times the amounts raised by Patty, Paula and me – his campaign picked up serious traction.

Richards began his attack on me, personally, by accusing me, in a letter to the Editor of the Holy Cross *Pine Nut*, of accepting campaign contributions from "outside interests" in Chicago.

In fact, my campaign had accepted a one hundred-dollar check from the Hon. Jack Keleher, a Cook County Judge whose son, Sean, had married my sister Elizabeth. Judge Keleher was one of the most respected members of the Bench in Chicago, and was as close to me as my father-in-law, Clark Grace.

So technically, I had accepted a contribution from someone in Chicago. But it was a contribution that made me proud, not ashamed, and the imputation of impropriety was ridiculous.

But perceptions can be fatal in politics, and as the campaign was coming to a conclusion, it was obvious that the new "slate" running against us moving ahead of us, and might very well prevail.

Ultimately, it did.

On the night of the election, Patty, Paula and I were ousted from office by a slate that hadn't played fair, but which did a better job than we did at communicating with our constituents.

It was painful, of course, and I didn't like being ousted on the basis of falsehoods and innuendo.

But the citizens of Holy Cross had spoken, and after six years, I was out of office.

Life is not always fair, of course, and as you will see in the chapter that follows, liars sometimes make bad things happen to good people.

Chapter 20

Father Brian

If you have read *Bless Me Father* you would know that I was raised as a Catholic. And for good or ill, I remain attached (more or less) to that ancient faith. Which is not to say that I'm not critical of many of its non-essential (in my view) teachings, which account for much of the nuttiness that surrounds the Church.

For example, I think it is ridiculous that Catholic priests are still not allowed to marry, after centuries when that was perfectly permissible. And that women are denied access to the priesthood. And that the Church officially bans birth control, even for couples where one of the partners has AIDS.

But I'll leave the politics of Catholicism to others.

For me, the greatest thing about the Catholic Church is the fact that it has employed many decent (if not holy) men and women who have devoted their lives to the service of others.

When I was living in Sutterville, I was blessed with a long, friendly relationship with Father Charlie Farrell, an Irish priest, only ten years older than I, for whom I used to serve as an altar boy when I was in grammar school.

We remained friends as I grew older, and it was not unusual for us to visit one another, sharing gossip and a glass (or two) of stout, while watching a sporting event at the rectory of Sacred Heart Church.

He was and remains a very good friend, and he was as good a story teller as anyone I have met. He was also a great comfort when I lost my wife, Jane, and he would routinely take my children to the zoo or on pony rides, to give me a break from the challenge of being a single parent.

The problem, of course, was that he was a hard act to follow.

So when I moved to Holy Cross, and had to pick a new parish to attend with my family, I was surprised and delighted to learn that one of my fellow students, from the days when I was studying for the priesthood at a seminary near Sutterville, was now the pastor of my parish.

His name was Brian Towery, and he was – not to over-use the expression – one of the smartest people I have ever known. He had the gift of near-perfect recall, he was well read, and he could solve complicated math problems – much like my son, Joseph – in his head.

Best of all, he had a really good heart.

He was sometimes referred to as the "million dollar priest" because he was one of the few students who had actually been ordained after attending a new multi-million dollar seminary that had been built just outside Sutterville to train young men for the priesthood.

Brian's father had once been a priest, and his mother had once been a nun, so theirs was a marriage that should never have happened. But it did, and they produced three wonderful children.

When I first discovered that Brian was my pastor, I immediately connected with him, and we were soon sharing afternoons together, golfing, riding bikes, and playing tennis.

For two or three years we were quite close.

But one day, disaster struck.

I received a call from Brian late one evening. He told me he was at the Holy Cross jail, that he had been arrested for child molestation, and that he needed a lawyer.

I have never practiced criminal law, and so there was no way I could represent him. But I did locate someone who could, and I went down to the jail and bailed him out.

As he left the jail I asked him what was going on. He told me that he had been one of the chaperones at a parish-sponsored camping trip for fifth graders. In the course of the trip, one of the campers claimed that he had walked over to where she and eleven other girls were sleeping, that he was naked, that he had climbed into her sleeping bag with her, and that he had fondled her.

He gave me the girl's name, which I recognized because I knew her father and mother...both of whom had asserted complaints against the other for spousal abuse.

I told Brian what I thought, that the story sounded preposterous. And my initial reaction was confirmed when I learned two days later that the girl, who was eleven years old, had previously made similar claims against two other adults, both of which had been discounted by the authorities.

When I heard that, of course, I assumed that the allegations against Brian would go nowhere; that no district attorney in his or her right mind would prosecute him.

But I was wrong.

At the time there were several well-known molestation complaints pending against Catholic priests, and the deputy district attorney in charge of prosecutions in Holy Cross was more than eager to join in the fray.

It turns out that the Deputy D.A.'s sister had been denied an annulment by the Catholic Church, and that Brian had been a member of the tribunal that had made the decision in her case. But that fact – which was reported in the Holy Cross *Pine Nut* – was apparently insufficient to stop Brian from being prosecuted.

Sadly, there was a price to be paid.

Brian had been widely expected to be nominated as the Bishop of our diocese, and because of the charges that nomination never materialized.

But something far worse occurred on the day Brian was arraigned. Hours after that proceeding, Brian learned that his father had suffered a heart attack and had passed away while being transported to the hospital.

As you might expect, Brian's mother was inconsolable, and she attributed her husband's death to the charges against Brian.

Justice of sorts was done when Brian's case eventually went to trial.

His jury unanimously found that he was not guilty.

And when Mary Greenfield, a reporter for the Holy Cross *Pine Nut*, questioned the jurors about their verdict, they told her that the claims against Brian were simply not credible.

According to the jurors, it made no sense that a grown man would walk naked into the middle of a crowd of eleven year olds. And how could a man who was six feet four inches tall climb into a child's sleeping bag which was only four feet long and thirty inches wide?

In fact, they found the lurid story told by the little girl so unbelievable that they wondered whether the deputy district attorney could be prosecuted for asserting them.

Unfortunately, by the time he was acquitted, Brian's reputation was already ruined, and there was simply no way he would ever be able to advance in the Catholic Church.

So he left Holy Cross, and finished his days as a counselor in a home for the criminally insane.

As for the assistant district attorney who prosecuted the case against Brian, she was appointed a judge of the Holy Cross Superior Court.

Chapter 21

My Parents Begin to Fail

Shortly after Jane died, I noticed for the first time that both of my parents had begun to show signs of aging. This shouldn't have been a shock. After all, when I left Sutterville I continued to subscribe to that city's last remaining daily, *The Union*, and it was not uncommon for me to see the parents of my contemporaries listed on the obituary pages.

My father was still working, and I was still unable to beat him at golf. But he had begun to walk and speak quite slowly, and he no longer had the stamina to stay up late with his children at holiday gatherings.

My mother, who was only three years younger than he, was becoming increasingly forgetful. This was quite startling, because she was someone who could still remember lines from Shakespeare that she had learned when she was a teenager.

And I noticed that she would become angry over trivial matters, things that would never have bothered her in the past. This, too, was not what I was used to. She had always been one of the most gracious persons on earth, and although she was quite spirited, she was never one to strike out at family or friends.

I mentioned my observations to my father, and he admitted that he had noticed the same thing. But he chalked it up to the normal course of growing older, and he told me that he didn't feel there was anything to worry about.

But as time went on, even he had to admit that she wasn't herself.

Then, the unthinkable happened: she answered a jury summons, and was selected to serve as a potential juror on a capital murder case. Startled, my father called me and asked me what I thought he should do.

I didn't want to embarrass my mother, of course, but neither did I want her to be on a panel that sent someone to death row. The jury selection process was still going on at the time, so I decided to act immediately. I called the trial judge, who I knew fairly well, and explained the situation to her.

To her credit, she promised me she would take care of the situation, and the next day my mother was excused because of what the judge had told the panel was a "family emergency."

Fortunately, my mother never learned what had led to her being excused from the panel.

Unfortunately, my mother's mental state continued to deteriorate, and within a year her "forgetfulness" was obvious to nearly everyone.

It was clear to me that my mother would soon be unable to appreciate what was going on around her, and so I decided to take her and my dad on a trip to Europe. As I saw it, the stimulus of travel might be good for her, and, at the very least, it would give me one last chance to be with both of my parents, even if things were not the way they used to be.

When we were young, my parents would take my siblings and me on trips to exotic places that they thought would broaden our horizons.

By far, the most interesting of these was a vacation in

Australia, where we had family ties. We also traveled around California, and I still have fond memories of family visits to the Yosemite Valley, the California Gold Country, and snow trips and hiking in the Sierra Nevada Mountains.

But we had never been to Europe together, and I decided it would be fun to take my parents there.

I spoke with my father about it, and he cautioned me against taking on too much. So we decided to limit our travel to Ireland and the United Kingdom.

We began our trip by flying to London, which is a fascinating place, and the perfect destination to entertain Americans who, like my parents, loved Anglo-Irish history.

We ended up visiting all the usual tourist attractions, including the Tower of London, Westminster Abbey, and Whitehall.

We also took several day trips, including bus tours to Oxford and Blenheim Palace. It was wonderful, and my mother seemed energized by the experience. In fact, it seemed that she was taking in most, if not all, of what she was seeing.

Because she had once been an actress, I was not surprised that my mother was particularly fond of Stratford-upon-Avon. However, I was surprised that she could still recall stories about Shakespeare himself, including the fact that in his "last will and testament" he had bequeathed his wife his "second best bed." She thought that was hilarious.

And when we walked past a reconstruction of the old Globe Theater, she even managed to recite a few lines of advice for actors from Hamlet's speech to the players:

"Speak the speech, I pray you, as I pronounced it to you, trippingly on the tongue: but if you mouth it, as many of our players do, I had as lief the town-crier spoke my lines. Nor do not saw the air too much with your hand, thus; but use all gently: for in the very torrent, tempest, and, as I may say, whirlwind of your passion, you must acquire and beget a temperance that may give it smoothness."

All of this from someone whose brain was supposedly functioning on a limited level.

After England, our next stop was Shannon Airport in Limerick, which is not far from the ancestral home of the Ryan clan in Galway.

I have close friends in that part of Ireland.

In fact, I am the godfather of one of the two children of Lord and Lady Connelly, who live in Castle Banny, where Fiona Ayers still lives with her mother on the Castle's grounds.

So I decided to take my parents there, and put them up in the Castle.

But before I did so I telephoned ahead to Lord Connelly. I warned him that my mother's memory had faded rather dramatically, and that she might be confused about what was going on around her. He assured me that her condition was hardly unique, that he understood perfectly, and he offered to throw a party for my parents and me when we arrived at the Castle.

As we approached Newmarket-on-Fergus, after a short flight from London, I explained to my parents that we would be staying at a castle, and that Fiona, who was much loved by them, would be there to greet us.

And sure enough, as we drove onto the Castle grounds, I could see that perhaps thirty or forty people had gathered on the front porch of its manor house. We immediately joined the festivities, which were hosted by Lord and Lady Connelly, and together we had one of the most elegant and enjoyable afternoons I have ever experienced.

After introducing my parents to Lord and Lady Connelly, and after working the crowd for a few minutes, I was taken aside by Fiona, who looked terrific and was all hugs, and I brought her up to date on my children.

I had done so for about half an hour when Lord Connelly interrupted us and pointed to a group of his friends that had gathered a few feet away from us.

There stood my mother, surrounded by perhaps a dozen of Lord Connelly's guests. And to my amazement, she was telling them stories and handling herself the way she used to when I was growing up – endlessly charming, and always the center of attention.

Lord Connelly smiled at me.

"You told me your mother was slipping away, and that she would be confused. Well, it seems to me that she is just fine, and that she is more than holding her own. In fact, we are not so much worried about her as we are about you." And they weren't worried about me.

It was true. It was as though my mother was transformed into her old self by the setting at Castle Banny.

Unfortunately, her transformation was short-lived.

That night Lord Connelly hosted a small dinner for my parents and me at nearby Bunratty Castle, a ruined edifice that had been converted into a restaurant, and was now a major tourist attraction.

After a wonderful four course dinner, which included wine and dessert, my mother turned to me and confided: "I love it here in Holy Cross."

I realized then that she had crossed back to the other side.

Chapter 22

Losing My Mother

Twelve months later my mother's condition had gotten far worse. Often times she couldn't remember the names of my children, and she had been forced to stop playing bridge, which was her lifelong passion.

Things came to a head one evening while I was in Washington D.C. visiting Maura and Joseph. My father called me at my hotel, and told me that my mother had gone outside for a walk, and hadn't returned. I asked him if he had called the police, which he had, but he said that several hours had already passed, and he was frightened that she was in trouble.

In the middle of our conversation there was a loud knocking at my father's front door. He answered it immediately, of course, and it turned out that the police had found my mother at a nearby shopping center. She had been confused, had been unable to identify herself, and couldn't give her address to the police. Fortunately, a friend of hers saw my mother being questioned, and he identified her for the police. And so, she was returned home safe.

The problem, of course, was what would have happened had she been injured? Or if my father hadn't noticed she was gone. Or if he hadn't called the police as soon as he did. Or if she hadn't been identified by her friend.

Clearly, something drastic had to happen.

My five siblings and I met with my father in Sutterville a few days later.

When we started our discussion, my father was adamant that he could handle the situation. But for the first time in my life, I could tell that he was frightened. And I knew that if anything bad happened to my mother he would blame himself.

Together, we all discussed the alternatives.

Not unexpectedly, my sister Mary, who is as selfless as anyone I know, offered to take in both of my parents, and let them stay at her house. But the rest of us said no. She had children of her own, and it made no sense to turn her home into an advanced care facility.

We also talked about sending full time care givers into my parents' home. But that, too, didn't make much sense. My father was adamant that he didn't want anybody living with him and my mother. And if he was unwilling to cooperate, the situation would only get worse.

So we ended up doing the one thing that we all said we would never do: we placed my mom in Aquinas House, an advanced care facility run by the Catholic Church to treat patients with Alzheimer's disease.

In some respects it was awful.

As might be expected, all of its patients had serious forms of dementia, although some were far worse than others. There was a strange odor throughout the place, a combination of bleach and feces, and there were constant moans from people who couldn't remember words, or how to pronounce them.

But in other respects it was beautiful. The staff was warm, engaging, and uniformly lovely. They took a deep, personal interest in all of their charges, and were as loving as anyone could hope for.

The individual rooms and the common areas were all spotlessly clean, and there were books and magazines everywhere; although the only patient I ever saw reading a magazine was holding it upside down.

Unfortunately, Aquinas House was located fifteen miles north of Sutterville, and my father had to drive his car that entire distance if he wanted to see my mother.

But drive it he did, every single day.

Whenever I'm on a freeway, and I see an old man driving along at forty-five miles an hour, instead of at the posted limit of seventy, I think of my father and I refuse to do what many people used to do when they saw him: honk their horn and shout insults.

Instead, I think about how much he loved my mother, about how he would do anything so see her, and about how he would spend six to eight hours every single day, helping out the staff at Aquinas House.

Eventually, when she could no longer recognize who he was, and she had lost her ability to speak, he would talk to her as lovingly as he always had, as though she understood everything he said and as though she was as lovely and bright as ever.

Then, one day in the spring of 1993, she died.

For my father, it was as though all the life inside him had disappeared.

I was trying a case in nearby Placerville at the time, and when I got the news I immediately headed for Aquinas House.

For I Have Sinned

When I arrived, my mother was lying on the top of her bed. Her eyes and mouth were open, and she was covered with moisture--as though she had been sweating. My father was sitting next to her in a stiff wooden chair, his eyes filled with tears. He was holding her hand, and he wouldn't let go.

He wouldn't speak, even to greet me.

A fellow patient at Aquinas House was floating in and out of my mother's room like some sort of ethereal being, and when she saw me she moaned and shook her head erratically.

I tried to comfort my father, but he wouldn't speak.

Finally, after I had been there for almost an hour, my brother Patrick arrived with a representative of a nearby funeral home, and he was finally able to pull my father away so that her body could be taken to a mortuary.

I placed a call to my old friend, our Parish Priest, Father Charlie Farrell, who was now the pastor emeritus of Sacred Heart Catholic Church, and I told him that my mother had died. His immediate response was to ask how my father was taking it. He ended our conversation with an observation. In his words, "he won't last long without her."

I wanted to dispute what he said, but I didn't. I knew he was right.

A week later I attended a beautiful funeral mass for my mother at Sacred Heart Church.

It's hard when you lose somebody who has lost their mind. In fact, my father sat through the ceremony looking as though he was shell shocked.

I tried to talk to him about his feelings, but he simply shook his head, and kept repeating that she was "a love."

In my case, and in my heart of hearts, I had to admit that a part of me had actually wanted her to die before she did. I wanted her to stop suffering, and to escape from the hell she was experiencing every day.

So I was surprised that I took her death as hard as I did.

I was one of several family members who delivered eulogies at her funeral, and although I am used to public speaking, it was very hard to talk about her.

After all, you only have one mother, and her loss was devastating.

But I was consoled by the large number of people who showed up.

This contrasted with recent experience with my parents' contemporaries. I had attended several funerals where the number of people in the main chapel was smaller than the number of people in the private "family" box which was curtained off in the area adjacent to the coffin of the deceased.

After her service, there was a reception at the Community Center of Sacred Heart Church.

It's all bit of a blur at this point, but I was able to catch up with many people I hadn't seen since I moved with my children to Holy Cross.

One of the people who impressed me most was a young Marine who had married one of my brother Patrick's two daughters. We spoke at length about the fact that his generation didn't seem to have the same sense of duty that my generation had; though I had to admit that my decision to serve as a Naval officer during the Vietnam War had been something less than enthusiastic.

Naturally, we spoke about his next assignment, and he told

me he would be going to Iraq.

In fact, he did so, and less than a month later I learned from my brother that he had been killed by a roadside bomb while he was riding in a convoy near Baghdad.

So a week after that, I was attending another funeral in Sutterville.

My father attended the funeral, and we spoke briefly. I asked him if he was doing okay, and he shrugged. It turned out that this was the last time I would ever see him.

I wish I had known that.

But I was grateful for one thing.

About a decade earlier I had heard a sermon from my old friend, Father Charlie Farrell. One of the things Father Charlie said in that sermon was that he had very few regrets in his life. But he did have one major regret that he would take to his grave. He regretted the fact that he had never told his father that he loved him.

I was very touched by that sermon and by that statement, and I took it to heart.

So the next time I saw my father, as I was leaving our old family home, I told him that I loved him. I wasn't surprised when he didn't respond. Nor did he respond the next dozen or so times that I told him how I felt.

But then something remarkable happened. He began to say "I love you, too."

And for the next ten years, we always ended our visits or telephone conversations by expressing our love for one another. And when he was gone, I found it comforting that we had done so.

To this day, whenever I speak to my children, or, indeed, to any family member, I always end our conversation by telling them that I love them.

Chapter 23

Losing My Father

With my mother gone, my father stopped functioning.

There was also an issue with his personal safety.

We had been worried about him driving. In fact, I had cringed every time I thought about him driving to Aquinas House to visit my mother. Without belaboring the point, it isn't good to drive forty-five miles an hour on a freeway where the speed limit is seventy, and many drivers are doing eighty.

In any case, now that he wasn't making that trip anymore, I didn't want him to continue operating a motor vehicle.

So I had a conversation with him much like I had with my grandmother twenty-five years earlier.

She was ninety years old at the time, and she had recently side-swiped a truck during a heavy rainfall. After speaking with my father about the situation I sat down with her and told her that it was time for her to hand over her car keys.

She looked at me with a sad look in her eyes and said "I know you are right, but not being able to drive will mean that my life will change dramatically."

I told her I thought that was nonsense, and that she could rely on me, or my father, or even take a cab, whenever she needed to go somewhere.

But she never called me or my father, and she never called a cab.

In fact, she pretty much became a hermit after that, and she died less than a year later.

Now, more than two decades later, I told my father that it was time for him to hand over his car keys.

Like his mother, he told me that he knew I was right, but he was reluctant to give up his "social" life which now consisted of mixing it up with a crowd of regulars who attended daily mass at Sacred Heart Church, and of making daily trips to the local supermarket.

But he handed over his keys, and I was pleased that he did.

What I didn't know was that he had an extra set of keys hidden from all of us, and that he had no intention of giving up his daily routine.

And he didn't.

Then, not three months after my mother died, I received a call from my brother Patrick.

"Dad died a few minutes ago," he said.

It was a Saturday morning, and my father had been speaking to my sister Mary on the telephone from an assisted care facility where he had moved shortly after my mother died.

At some point during the conversation he had told Mary that he was feeling faint, that he was going to lie down, and that he would call her back in about five minutes.

When, an hour later, he hadn't called back, Mary called his facility, and asked the staff to check on him. They called her back a minute or two later, and told her that he'd had a heart attack and that they had called an ambulance. But by the time it arrived, he was gone.

At the time he died, he was in remarkably good shape for someone in his late eighties. It was just that the death of my mother had drained all the life out of him.

When my mother was younger, and still had her health, he would always defer to her on domestic matters. If one of their children needed permission for a trip, or needed some spending money, or wanted advice on a relationship, it was she, not he, who we would speak with.

But when she was sick, and had became a shadow of the person who had raised us, he had stepped up to take her place, and I had developed a relationship with him that enriched my years as an adult in ways I would never have anticipated. All of my siblings had similar experiences.

One of my last conversations with him took place at the funeral of my niece's husband, the Marine, and it concerned the fact that I was feeling lonely.

By then, Maura and Joseph had been out of the nest for several years, and he told me that he thought it was time that I move on. I asked him what he meant, and he told me that I needed a wife. I told him about my concerns for my children, and I repeated the advice he had given me about relationships many years earlier, "If you have to ask about a relationship, the answer is no."

He smiled when I said this, and he responded that it would be more appropriate to follow my mother's advice: "You need to find your great love."

In my mind, of course, I had already found my great love, but I didn't want to debate the matter with him.

In truth, I had to admit, at least to myself, that there were times when I was lonely, not simply alone, and I knew instinctively that I needed – and wanted – more than I had. So I promised him that I would think it over.

Then he died.

But I still considered what he had said, and for several days I looked back over the loves and losses I had experienced.

I eventually decided that I would do what I really hadn't done in decades. I would open myself to the possibility of a relationship – and to love.

But as they say in politics, the difficulty is in the details.

There were lots of women out there. But how many would I be interested in? And more important, how many would be interested in me?

I had two children, and in the dating world, children are considered baggage. Even when they were grown and long out of the house.

I was also living on the Central Coast, which is a beautiful place, but men who live there are widely seen in the outside world as being "GU," or geographically undesirable.

I wasn't about to become a barfly, and the notion of actively dating multiple women wasn't very appealing. But if someone came along, I promised myself I would be open to the possibility of a long-term relationship.

As it turned out, it was a good thing I didn't hold my breath.

Chapter 24

The Gerhardt Litigation

Once my parents were gone, I found myself thinking less about dating and more about immersing myself into the practice of law. Over the years, the nature of that practice usually involved commercial litigation of one kind or another.

Big or small, complex or simple, I found litigation invariably fascinating.

Not surprisingly, the most interesting part of litigation is the interplay between the principals who are fighting one another.

Some of my litigation clients have been easy to work with, and others, like Phil Parentini, have been challenging.

The most difficult of the latter was undoubtedly the CEO of a small steel fabricating company located in the San Joaquin Valley of Central California: Aram Kenoshian.

In the fall of 1990, a few months after I moved my practice to Holy Cross, I was asked to represent Kenoshian Steel Incorporated, or KSI. KSI had contracted with a German company, Gerhardt AG, to fabricate heavy duty cranes that would be used to load and unload cargo ships in Seattle.

Six cranes were ultimately delivered to Seattle by KSI, but the Port Authority there had rejected all of them on the ground that there were cracks in the struts, and that these defects could lead them to collapse during cargo operations.

Gerhardt sued Kenoshian in San Francisco Federal Court, alleging that KSI had manufactured the struts for the cranes using cheap steel it had imported from Hong Kong.

Kenoshian counter-claimed, arguing that there was nothing wrong with its steel, and that the real problem lay with the strut design supplied by Gerhardt.

The defense of Kenoshian in the Gerhardt lawsuit had originally been referred to my father-in-law, Clark Grace, of the Grace Law Firm, but it turned out they had a conflict of interest, so Clark referred the matter to me.

I knew that the lawsuit would tie me up for months, if not years, and I was reluctant to take it on by myself. So I called a friend of mine, Mel Richtel, who practices law in Fresno, and who happens to speak German.

Together we decided to take on Gerhard, and thus began a four year adventure that had us traveling around the world, taking hundreds of depositions, and ultimately, trying a month-long jury trial before a federal judge in San Francisco.

As we prepared for trial it seemed to me that the facts, which were undisputable in several important respects, favored our side.

Gerhardt had, in fact, prepared the specifications for the failed struts, and there were in-house memoranda generated by Gerhardt engineers which had warned of potential metal fatigue due to their specs, and which predicted the cranes would fail if they were not re-engineered. The cranes had not been re-engineered.

But Mel and I had discovered a problem on our side; a problem which had not been discovered by Gerhardt.

As part of our preparation for trial, Mel and I hired an independent lab to test the scrap metal that Kenoshian had used to fabricate the struts. The tests indicated that the metal was, in fact, contaminated by a particle that could cause it to fail under pressure.

Our independent tests contradicted earlier results generated by Gerhardt and the supplier in Hong Kong. Worse still for our side, our tests detailed specific identical mistakes made by the laboratories who had conducted those earlier tests by Gerhardt and the Hong Kong supplier.

In other words, Mel and I had generated and paid for an expert report that could destroy our case.

It probably bears noting that the American legal system is grounded on the notion that each side in a civil dispute puts on its best case, and that neither side is obligated to assist the other.

But there is a conflicting notion that is basic to the way the system works: attorneys are also officers of the Court.

In other words, an attorney must never make a representation to the Court which we know to be false. Or to put forth "facts" that we know not to be true.

Applying these principals, neither Mel nor I would be required to turn over the results of our metallurgical tests to Gerhardt. But ethically, we could not point to the tests that had been done by Gerhardt and the Hong Kong supplier, knowing that they were flawed.

This was fine in principle. But when Aram Kenoshian heard that we would not be relying on Gerhardt's tests, he went ballistic.

The first thing he did in response was to call Clark Grace, and complain to him. To his credit, Clark told him to relax and follow the advice of his counsel.

The second thing Kenoshian did was to file a complaint against Mel and me with the California Bar Association, but the Bar refused to intervene.

The third thing he did was fire Mel and me. This was problematic on several levels.

Neither Mel nor I had been paid for several months, and a fight over how much we would be paid upon leaving the Gerhardt lawsuit could be painful and expensive for both of us. Plus there was the question of who could (or would be willing to) take over the defense of the Gerhardt trial.

A solution finally came when Clark Grace sat down with Aram Kenoshian, and convinced him to rescind his decision to fire Mel and me.

I never knew what Clark said to change Kenoshian's mind, but about a week after Mel and I were canned, Kenoshian called me late one night (apparently under the influence of an intoxicant) and he apologized for acting "rashly."

We ended up winning the Gerhardt lawsuit, including hundreds of thousands of dollars in attorney's fees which were awarded to the "prevailing" party under the written contract between Gerhardt and Kenoshian.

It turned out that our "poor design" argument carried the day, and we never had to rely on the test results generated by the opposition.

So somehow or other the system worked.

At least it appeared to.

Chapter 25

The Butcher Litigation

Another case that caused me no end of grief over the years was a contract dispute that was as strange as it was challenging.

It involved differences between my client, Michael J. Capitini, and his former partner, Calvin Butcher.

Butcher was one of those guys who had all the trappings of wealth: a beautiful mansion on the beach; a brand new Bugatti; two attractive children who were enrolled in a prestigious prep school; a twin engine Beech Baron; a beautiful young wife; and a membership in the exclusive Holy Cross Beach and Tennis Club.

Butcher had charmed poor Michael into investing hundreds of thousands of dollars into the retrofit of an abandoned automobile parts warehouse just south of Holy Cross.

Michael was a very smart guy, and he had generated the money he used for his investment by making a series of shrewd real estate deals in and around the Central Coast.

Michael was also a pretty good judge of character, and he never suspected that his partner was a crook.

This time his judgement was off.

Butcher took all the money that Michael had invested, and he handed it over to a pension fund that was supposedly acting as the general contractor for the retrofit project. But before he did so, he deducted a "commission" of $25,000 which he kept for himself.

The pension fund then took the balance of Michael's money and spent it in all sorts of ways, none of which had anything to do with the retrofit.

Shortly thereafter work stopped on the retrofit, and the pension fund walked off the job.

When Michael asked Butcher why it had done so, Butcher told him that the pension fund hadn't been paid for the work it performed. And when Michael asked what happened to the money he had invested, Butcher told him that it was all gone.

Michael immediately hired me to represent him, and I filed a lawsuit against the pension fund and Butcher.

The first thing that happened after I filed suit was that there was a series of unexplained fires in and around Holy Cross.

One of the fires nearly destroyed the former parts warehouse, another broke out in Michael's garage, and another occurred in the trash can in my back yard.

You didn't have to be a genius to figure out what was going on, but I hired a private investigator to confirm my suspicions.

The investigator, Bob Byers, was a former FBI Agent. He was a tough guy, and very smart. He had fallen out of grace with the Bureau after one of his nemeses, a tribal leader who had been accused of killing another FBI agent, had been found dead at the bottom of a well on a reservation in southeastern Montana. Byers had been implicated in his death.

Nothing was ever proven, and Byers left the Bureau voluntarily, but under a cloud.

Within a week after Byers was on my payroll, he reported back to me that Butcher was behind the fires, and he had turned up enough evidence (including a statement from an eyewitness) that he thought the Holy Cross District Attorney could successfully prosecute Butcher for arson, and perhaps attempted murder.

But the District Attorney refused.

I found out later that Butcher had been a major donor to the District Attorney's campaign fund.

Byers was furious.

In fact, he told me wanted to engage in a little "self help" relative to Butcher, but I talked him out of it. "Let's get him in court," I argued, and we set out to do just that.

With the help of Byers, I spent two and a half years lining up witnesses, collecting statements and sorting through thousand of pages of evidence that I was convinced would lead to an award of punitive damages against both Butcher and the pension fund.

But at the last minute, the pension fund declared bankruptcy, and on that same day Butcher disappeared.

It turned out that in the months before he disappeared Butcher had filed a dissolution action against his wife, and as part of the divorce process he had set up a series of trusts to make sure that his wife and children kept their beautiful home, his airplane, and the bulk of his other possessions.

On the same day he had disappeared, he had also closed escrow on three separate bank loans for two million dollars each, all of which were secured by the same property: the home that was in the trust naming his wife and children as sole beneficiaries.

The loan money was immediately wired to a bank in the

Grand Cayman Islands, and then to a bank in Andorra, and then to a Swiss bank account, from which the money was withdrawn by a woman who was unknown to the bank, but who possessed the appropriate passwords to access the account.

The FBI was called in, of course, and although they initially refused to work with Byers, they eventually developed a plan to track down Butcher.

But he was nowhere to be found.

My lawsuit was derailed, obviously, and I had to hire a bankruptcy specialist, Henry Niles, to demand satisfaction from the pension fund, and to demonstrate that the "trusts" created by Butcher were a sham.

The matter eventually had a happy ending.

Butcher was captured in Monaco by Interpol, and he was returned to the United States. He was prosecuted for and convicted of bank fraud. At his trial he claimed he had spent all the money he had wired to Switzerland, and the government never did recover anything from him. After spending less than a year at a minimum security facility, he returned to Holy Cross, where he reunited with his wife and children.

The last time I saw him he was sitting in a hot tub at the Holy Cross Beach and Tennis Club. And he was hitting on a young Australian woman sitting with him in the hot tub, bragging to her about his world travels.

I noticed that he didn't mention he was being pursued by Interpol during those travels.

As for Michael, he and I were able to force the sale of Butcher's mansion, and he recovered about fifty percent of the losses he had suffered.

As for Byers, he ultimately decided he didn't want to be a private investigator any more. So he gave up his license, and together with his girlfriend he bought a country-western bar in nearby Hollister.

Chapter 26

Grate Expectations

While I was in law school, one of my professors told my class that, in his opinion, anybody who would choose to be a litigator probably had a personality disorder.

I can't speak to the truth of that opinion, but it is undeniable that the trial bar has many bizarre members.

Certainly, one of the most interesting of these in my experience was an old lawyer by the name of Harry Bach. As a child, Harry had moved to Holy Cross from Berlin, Germany, and by the time I moved to Holy Cross he had a reputation for being outrageous.

His suits were always rumpled, his shirts were always stained, and he never wore socks.

He also openly flaunted the legal canons of ethics.

Twice he was censured by the California Bar for paying off ambulance drivers for "referring" injured patients to him. And you could never leave a legal file in a place where he could lay his hands on it, because he would read it if you left the room.

He would do anything, honest or crooked, to win and for that reason he was ostracized by his fellow lawyers, including myself.

So you can imagine how I felt when I learned that he had

been retained to represent a co-defendant of my client in a civil suit for breach of contract.

The suit had been filed by Peter Gillette, a defrocked physician representing himself *in propria persona* who operated a non-profit cancer research facility in Southern California. The named defendants in the suit were my client (and good friend), Donny LeBlanc, and Bach's client, an automobile restoration business doing business as Phoenix Found, Incorporated or "PFI."

According to Gillette, Donny had damaged him by "conspiring" with PFI to destroy his aging Rolls-Royce. The alleged mechanism for that destruction was restoring it with defective after-market parts that "forever damaged the integrity and value" of his "venerable classic automobile."

I decided to avoid Harry Bach as much as I could, and what limited "discovery" I did was conducted independent of Bach; so I wouldn't be associated with him.

We ultimately tried the case before a jury in the old Holy Cross courthouse, and I can honestly say that it was one of the oddest trials I have ever experienced.

Mr. Gillette's opening statement rambled on for almost two hours, and as far as I could tell his only complaint against Donny was that he had loaned money to PFI.

At the end of his statement, I asked the judge to dismiss the case outright against my client, but she refused to do so. According to her, Mr. Gillette was entitled to a "break" because of his *pro per* status.

In fact, and as a matter of law, Mr. Gillette was legally obligated to meet the same obligations that are required of attorneys. But the truth is that judges routinely allow people who represent themselves to get away with things that would never be sanctioned if they were done by a licensed attorney.

After my motion to dismiss was denied, I made a short opening statement. I noticed that the members of the jury were nodding their heads as I spoke, and I felt I was making progress.

Then Mr. Bach addressed the jury.

If it was possible, his statement was even less coherent than that of Mr. Gillette. And from the looks on the faces of the jurors, Mr. Bach was about to snatch defeat from the jaws of victory.

I could tell from the look on the faces of his client's principals, the PFI owners, that they were confused and upset with Bach, but there was nothing they could do about it at that point.

After that, the trial went fairly well from my perspective.

The judge had limited the testimony of the witnesses to matters that were relevant. And early the following afternoon the case went to the jury.

About an hour into its deliberations, one of the sheriff's deputies, who was a courtroom bailiff, walked into the men's lavatory on the second floor of the courthouse, and found Bach lying on the floor. The deputy asked Bach if he was all right. Bach looked startled, and he told the deputy that he had simply passed out.

But the deputy was suspicious.

After Bach left the lavatory, the deputy walked over to the place where Bach had been lying, and he lay down in the same spot. And to his astonishment, he could hear voices coming from a grate near the floor where Bach's head had been.

He realized that the voices were coming from the jury room downstairs, and that Bach had been listening in to their deliberations.

The deputy immediately reported his discovery to our trial judge. And a half hour later, the judge declared a mistrial.

Bach was also told he could no longer represent PFI, and that he would be reported to the Bar.

As a practical matter, this meant that we would have to try the Gillette case all over again.

I had no problem doing so, since Gillette's presentation had demonstrated that he had no case. And I was happy that Bach would no longer be involved in the case.

Unfortunately, PFI no longer had a lawyer, and I learned that it principals didn't have the money to hire one.

I had no moral or legal obligation to pick up the pieces of their failed attorney-client relationship with Bach, but I had gotten to know them during the trial, and I thought they were good people.

The principals were two young women, Cheryl Harris and Lynn Irvin, who had been married to the original owners of PFI, and were now roommates living in Southern California. They had acquired their interests in PFI in divorce settlements after they had both been dumped – virtually simultaneously – by their respective spouses, who had run off with two Chilean flight attendants they had met while on a business junket to Aruba.

I felt they had been treated shabbily by their counsel, so I told Cheryl and Lynn that I would help them out for free, at least to the extent that I could do so without violating the canons of ethics.

Which I did.

But there was never a retrial.

A month later, on the morning we were set to pick a new jury, Gillette failed to show up for our trial, and the trial judge granted my motion to dismiss the claims against both Donny and PFI.

As we left the Courthouse, I invited Donny, Cheryl and Lynn to join me for lunch.

They all agreed, and as was my custom after a victory, we had lunch at the Coop Room.

I remember that Billy Burns, the bartender at the Coop Room, called me aside at some point during our lunch, and he remarked about how happy Donny and I seemed in the company of these ladies.

Certainly I was.

In fact, the ladies were very special people, and I was gratified, and happy, that I had been able to get them off the legal hook without their having to spend money for a defense they could not otherwise afford.

But there was something else going on as well.

Our time together that afternoon seemed to fly by, and it seemed that we were constantly laughing – to the point that at least one disgruntled patron told Billy that she wanted to complain about us to the Coop Room's management.

Needless to say, Donny was amused by the request, and no censure was issued by him – the management.

I couldn't help but notice that Lynn, in particular, seemed to be responding to me in ways that made me feel both special, and somewhat apprehensive. I was experiencing the kind of attention I hadn't felt in years, but on reflection I decided that whatever was happening was long overdue.

Chapter 27

Lynn

The day after our victory lunch, I invited Lynn and Cheryl over to my house for dinner. Lynn agreed to come, but Cheryl wasn't feeling well, so she stayed at Lynn's parents' house in Holy Cross.

Jane' sister, Peggy, was also in town, so I invited her.

Donny LeBlanc joined us as well.

The meal was supposed to be a celebration of our victory, so I opened up two old bottles of champagne that had been sitting around my house for years. Thy had been given to me by my parents, and had been acquired by them to celebrate the defeat of Richard Nixon in his failed attempt to be elected governor of California in 1962.

In the course of our celebration, as the four of us finished off the champagne – which was more noteworthy for its history than its taste – I noticed that Donny was paying special attention to Peggy. At the end of the evening, he was holding her hand.

Obviously, something was going on between them, so I wasn't surprised when I heard him ask her if she would join him as his guest at a political fundraiser he was hosting at the Holy Grail the next day.

But that wasn't the only thing going on.

The excitement and ambivalence – now curiosity – I had felt about Lynn the day before was still coursing through me like a pleasant shock of electricity.

At the end of the evening I said something I could hardly believe I was saying. I told Lynn that I thought I might be falling in love.

Lynn was in her mid 40's; pretty, smart and athletic. She was also an artist. She took from her purse miniature copies of some of her paintings. They were reminiscent of the young Edward Hopper; think "The Nighthawks" – only better.

As a practical matter, I was having trouble keeping my eyes off her.

For the past decade and a half, when she wasn't overseeing her automobile restoration business with Cheryl, Lynn had worked as a sales representative for a large pharmaceutical company. She traveled frequently, and was a regular visitor to Holy Cross. Her parents had lived in the village since her father had retired from the Air Force five years earlier as a three-star general. Her mother had been a graphic artist.

Her twin sister, who was her best friend, had died of breast cancer several years earlier.

The death of her sister, and the pain caused by the breakup of her marriage, had left her emotionally fragile. But she was fun to be with, she loved children, and I found myself drawn to her in ways that I hadn't experienced with any woman for years.

The biggest down side with Lynn was that she lived in West Hollywood – which was a seven hour drive (without traffic) from Holy Cross.

But she was lovely, and frankly, the more we talked, the more I wanted to be around her.

The day after the dinner at my place, I gave myself a day off, and I took Lynn and Cheryl on a three-and-a-half hour hike through a nearby redwood grove and, later to one of my favorite beaches on Monterey Bay.

Along the way we took photographs of one another. When I printed out one that Cheryl had taken of Lynn and me near the entrance to Old Brighton State Park, I couldn't help but think of the similarity between that photo and the photo of my grandparents taken when they were on their first date.

After Lynn and Cheryl returned to Southern California, I found myself daydreaming about Lynn. Before I knew it I had called her and asked her if I could visit her.

To my surprise and great pleasure, she said she thought that would be a great idea, and two weekends later, early on a Friday morning, I found myself driving to West Hollywood.

When I arrived, Lynn greeted me and told me that Cheryl was out of town on business, and would be unable to join us. I was grateful, but didn't dare say so. For the next three days we had a magical time together.

The first thing that struck me about Lynn's world was the sheer beauty of her artwork. She had perhaps a dozen of her paintings on display in her apartment, and they were far more impressive than the miniature photos of her paintings that she had shown me while she was in Holy Cross.

The second thing that struck me was the depth of her personality. When she wasn't around Cheryl, she displayed an interest in philosophy and even politics that I hadn't seen before, and it took me by surprise.

The continuing chemistry between us was palpable and unmistakable. I found myself being drawn closer and closer to her.

At some point I decided there was no doubt. I was in love. Not since Jane's death had I entertained such thoughts, and I didn't know what to do about it.

I wasn't sure I wanted to broach the subject with Jane's sister. I was afraid there might be some sensitivity there. So I decided to go to my friends, Patty Gambino and Paula Croatia, for advice. Quite sensibly, they told me they wanted to meet Lynn, and that they would give me their impressions about her after they had a chance to speak with her.

An opportunity to do just that came a month later. There was a fund raiser at the Coop Room, and I took Lynn, who was visiting her parents for the weekend, as my guest.

This was our first opportunity to get together since I had traveled to see her in West Hollywood, and was my first "formal date" in years. Patty and Paula saw me arrive with Lynn, and shortly thereafter the process of vetting Lynn began.

Indeed, I held my breath when I saw the three of them talking for what seemed like an hour or more.

The next morning there was a message from Patty on my answering machine asking me to meet her and Paula for lunch at the Coop Room. We met, and the reaction of both women was unambiguous: "Marry this woman," they said. "She is a treasure."

My father advised me years ago that you should never ask for advice if you are not willing to follow it. In this case, it seemed to me, the advise of Patty and Paula was sound.

The next day I spoke to my children, who happened to be home, and I told them I wanted them to meet someone special. They immediately figured out what was going on and they told me they wanted to meet Lynn right away.

When they did so, it was like a love fest.

So Lynn and I began dating.

Our original arrangement had me traveling to West Hollywood two weekends every month, and Lynn traveling to Holy Cross on the other two weekends.

I have to admit that I had been somewhat naive about the difficulty of maintaining a relationship with someone who lived a seven-hour drive away, but we kept this up for almost a year.

Finally, I asked her to marry me.

To my relief, but not great surprise, and clear delight, she said she would.

The first thing she did after we became engaged was to quit her job with the pharmaceutical company she had worked at for almost a decade, and she sold her interest in PFI to her friend Cheryl.

Shortly after that she moved to Holy Cross, and with the help of Maura, planned a quiet wedding at my parish church.

In August of 1998 we were married.

Peggy and Donny LeBlanc, who had announced their own engagement a month earlier – that had been some dinner that night at my house – acted as maid of honor and best man, and we had a small reception at The Holy Grail.

For me it was an exceptionally happy time, and it was as though my life had begun all over again.

Little did I realize how dramatically things were about to change.

Chapter 28

My Life With Lynn

Once we were married, Lynn moved quickly to settle in.

She made a suggestion that made a lot of sense. She told me that she wanted us to focus on activities that would help us grow as a couple.

One of the first things we decided to do in that regard was to have a standing "date" every Friday evening. And naturally we chose the bar at the Coop Room for our weekly rendez-vous.

We established a routine early on.

We would meet at 6:00 p.m., and start by sharing a bottle of red Pinot brought to us by our faithful bartender, Billy Burns.

Billy would then bring us an order of grilled calamari, and we would finish our meal with vanilla ice cream covered with strawberries.

Billy was a classic bartender, dispensing wisdom and sage advice as well as food and drinks. We would also mix with the regulars who made the Coop Room a nightly stop.

One Friday evening, May 14, 1999, almost nine months to the day after we were married, I was running a little late, and I met Lynn at the Coop Room at about 6:15.

When I arrived, Lynn was drinking sparkling water, and

For I Have Sinned

Billy brought us a bottle of our "usual" Pinot. But then something strange happened. Lynn told me she wouldn't be drinking any of the wine, and she asked Billy for another bottle of sparkling water.

Our love of fine wines was something Lynn and I had in common, so I asked her if she was all right.

Her answer floored me.

"Actually, I'm pregnant," she said.

I asked her how that was possible. After all, she was in her mid-forties at the time, and I knew she had been having night flashes.

I didn't think it was possible to conceive a child at that age.

Lynn smiled, and shook her head. "Jay, I checked with my gynecologist. It's official. I'm pregnant. The only thing I don't know is whether we will be having a boy or a girl."

So I kissed Lynn, gave her a hug, and then I drank the entire bottle of Pinot.

Chapter 29

Pregnancy

For the next nine months, things were hectic and stressful in the Ryan household.

We cleared out some of the furniture from Maura's bedroom, and brought in a crib and changing table. I also made several trips to a box store in San Jose, buying car seats, blankets, cuddly toys, and other accessories that we would need to care for a new baby.

We were delighted when my children told me how happy they were about the prospect of a new sibling.

My friends and family – especially Lynn's parents – were not only supportive but joyful. And Clark and Auntie Peggy sent over boxes and boxes of toys and formula.

But I was nervous.

Lynn would still be in her mid-forties by the time she gave birth, and I knew that the chances of a birth defect were quite high for baby whose mother was that age.

I wasn't exactly young myself. I was in my fifties at the time, and I had read a number of articles that pointed out the hazards of women – even younger women – becoming impregnated by older men.

Lynn proved to be a trooper notwithstanding the odds. She went to see her OB-GYN every other week, and she had dozens of tests. Incredibly, delightfully, they all came back normal.

In the sixth month of Lynn's pregnancy we learned that we were having a girl. Lynn showed incredible sensitivity to my children and to Jane's family by suggesting that we name our little girl after my late wife.

But a cloud appeared.

When Lynn was in her seventh month of pregnancy, she woke me one morning and told me she was having cramps and was experiencing vaginal bleeding.

I thought to myself that I should have expected this, given Lynn's and my ages, and I was angry with myself for expecting so much from a high-risk pregnancy.

I drove Lynn down to the Holy Cross Hospital, and I asked for Lynn's OB-GYN, but it was a weekend, and she was not on call.

After we waited for what seemed an eternity, an obstetrical nurse took Lynn into an emergency room examination area for tests.

About an hour later, the nurse came outside to speak with me. To put it mildly I was not eager to hear what she had to say, reckoning that the news would not be good.

"I guess you better give me the news," I said reluctantly.

The nurse gave me a broad smile, and said:

"What is the matter with you? You have a healthy little girl who is going to be just fine. Here. Take a look at this."

We walked into the examination room where Lynn was getting dressed, and she showed me a film clip that was apparently taken by a device that could record images and movement inside someone's womb.

And sure enough, I could make out the features of our little girl, kicking her legs and swinging her arms. It was simply beautiful, and I started tearing up.

One month later I was on the East Coast meeting clients in connection with a business dispute. I had received a call from Lynn, but my phone had been powered off at the time and so she left a message.

"My OB-GYN says I'm contracted four to five centimeters. Jane will be born today. Get back here immediately."

Of course, I cancelled my meeting, and I caught a series of flights that almost got me back in time for the birth. I missed it by about three hours.

After my final flight, I took a cab from the San Jose airport to Holy Cross, and made the trip in record time.

When I arrived at the hospital I ran up the stairs to the hospital nursery, and I was greeted by Maura – who had arrived in Holy Cross a day earlier so she could attend the wedding of a friend. As you can imagine, memories of losing my first wife during childbirth flooded my brain. But thankfully, Maura assured me that both Lynn and the baby were fine.

Nervously, I asked Maura about the baby's APGAR score, which is a scale with a low of 1 to a high of 10 which is used by hospitals to assess the heath of newborns.

Maura laughed, amused, I suppose, that I knew what an APGAR score was, but understanding my concerns.

"She's fine dad," she said. "She's a perfect 10."

Maura took me to Lynn's room, and there they were: mother and daughter, as beautiful as any two people on the planet.

I was incredibly happy that night, and I still smile when I

think about the scene in Lynn's room as she and Maura passed little Jane back and forth. But my joy was tempered by my knowledge that it would be a challenge for Lynn and me to raise a child who was so much younger than we were.

I recalled a line I remember by the English poet, William Blake, that contrasted the joy of birth with the hazards of the world outside. In his words, "My mother groaned, my father wept, and into the dangerous world I leapt."

I silently prayed that the life of my little Jane – or Janie as everyone would eventually call her – would be measured more by her joy than by the hazards she would face in life.

Instead of Blake, I would prefer to think of Shakespeare's line from *Midsummer Night's Dream*, "Though she be but little, she is fierce!"

If you would indulge me, I'd like to quote a bit more Wordsworth: "Thou child of joy, shout round me, let me hear thy shouts..."

I did, gladly, hear those shouts.

The truth was that my life could only be transformed for the good by this addition to our family, and I hoped along with my prayer that I would be up to the task of being a good father to this beautiful child.

Chapter 30

Janie

After raising two children, and reaching an age where one would normally expect to be a grandparent, not the parent of a newborn, it was a shock to find myself changing diapers, waking up in the middle of the night to warm up formula, and addressing the challenges that all new parents experience, but which most parents forget about by the time their child reaches age one.

As a child of middle-aged parents, Janie didn't stand a chance of growing up like her siblings.

When Jane and I were raising Maura, and especially I as a single parent during the first few years after Jane had died, I was always strapped for money.

But by the time Janie came along, I was a successful attorney. I traveled often, and whenever I could I would bring Lynn and Janie along with me.

Because of this, by the time Janie was seven years old she had been to the East Coast so often that when we visited the National Zoo in Washington D.C., she could lead me to all of her favorite animals without the benefit of a map or signs.

If she wanted shoes – which she did from her earliest years to the point that I sometimes referred to her as Imelda – she got shoes. And if she wanted a doll house, she got a doll house. In fact, she pretty much got anything she wanted.

Lynn cautioned me about spoiling her, but amazingly, she turned out to be as loving and generous a child as one could imagine.

Let me give you a few examples.

First, the summer after Janie finished pre-school, when she was four, the two of us were in a park near our home. Janie was playing on a slide. As she did so, a woman and her child came into the park, and her little boy started speaking with Janie. While this was going on, his mother approached me, and asked if Janie was my daughter. I told her she was, and the woman responded by telling me a story. According to her, she and her husband were both Korean, and they were in the process of finishing up a one-year teaching assignment at nearby San Jose State University. At the beginning of their assignment they had placed their son in the same pre-school Janie was attending, but unfortunately, he spoke no English. The little boy was afraid to go to pre-school because he spoke only Korean. But he was all smiles when she picked him up at the end of his first day of school. A little girl, Janie, had apparently befriended him, and had promised to teach him English. And for that entire school year she made it a point each day to spend time with him and teach him words, and ultimately sentences. Janie couldn't speak Korean, of course, but she would read him picture books and help him with his pronunciation. After telling me this, the woman told me that Janie was the best thing that happened to her son in America, and that one of her few regrets she and her husband had about returning to Korea was that her son would no longer have Janie to help him learn.

Second, several years later, while Janie was in the third grade, Lynn and I were staying at a hotel in Santa Monica, where a cousin of Maura and Joseph was getting married. When we woke up on the last morning of our stay in Southern California, and were preparing to check out, Janie told me she wanted have breakfast at a fast food restaurant which she had seen across from our hotel. I said okay, and we walked over to the restaurant, which was adjacent to the Santa Monica Pier. When we entered the restaurant I could see that there were a few paying customers, but that most of the people who were sitting down were homeless people who had gone inside to protect themselves from a particularly brisk morning. Janie's mother and I had always told her that she should be generous with the homeless, and so I was not entirely surprised when she asked me to give her some dollar bills for the "poor people." I ended up cashing a twenty dollar bill, and I handed her twenty singles. She then walked around the restaurant, and gave one of the dollars to each of the homeless persons she saw there. In fact, she ran out of the first twenty bills I had given her, and she insisted that I cash another ten so she could help out several people she had missed.

And third, more recently, while she was in the seventh grade, Janie volunteered each week to work at a shelter for battered women in downtown Holy Cross. One afternoon, as I was waiting in my car to drive Janie to the shelter, she emerged from our house carrying a large cardboard box full of clothing. I asked her what she was doing, and she told me she was donating the clothing to the shelter. I helped her load the box into the back of my car, and as I did so I noticed that a new parka her mother and I had given her for her birthday, as well as several of her favorite dresses, had been neatly packed inside. I asked her if the parka and dresses no longer fit her, but she shook her head. "They fit me fine, daddy," she said, "but there are girls at the shelter who need them more than I do."

This was the kind of good heart that Lynn and I had hoped for when Janie was born, and we were not to be disappointed.

Chapter 31

Rome

Eventually, Maura and Joseph began producing children of their own, and with Janie about to enter high school, Lynn and I decided that we wanted to do a lot more traveling than we had in the past.

We had both traveled often in connection with our jobs, but we hadn't visited the kinds of places I had enjoyed as a student in Europe or during my service in Asia as a Naval officer.

Certainly my favorite destination was Italy, and I told Lynn I wanted to go there with her while we were both still young enough to enjoy it.

As a student in Rome, I recall thinking how sad it was to see tourist buses filled with people (mostly women) who were too frail to climb (or even walk) around the ancient sites that I found most interesting. I wasn't going to let that happen to us.

In the spring of 2012, after Janie graduated from grammar school, Lynn and I booked a month long visit to Rome.

Clark and Auntie Peggy agreed that Janie could stay with them during our trip, and Lynn and I were excited to spend some quality time alone in Europe.

Rome is very beautiful, of course, but it is also complex. I think it is impossible to get to know the city by visiting it for just a few days, or even a few weeks.

But after living there for a full academic year in the 1960's, I felt like I had a pretty good feel for the place. And I felt I knew enough about its fountains, its churches, its piazzas, its ruins, its monuments, and its people that I could show Lynn around; to give her a sense of the only large city I really love.

During our first week in Rome, we staked out a series of morning and afternoon hikes that took us from our hotel near the Spanish Steps to sites like the Pantheon (my favorite structure in the world), the Roman Forum, Saint Peter's, and, of course, the Coliseum.

One of these walks, and certainly my favorite, was an morning-long visit to the Vatican Museum. That Museum, which is more than five hundred years old, and which consists of more than fifty separate galleries, including the Sistine Chapel, houses some of the most fascinating artwork and other exhibits in the world.

Michelangelo's depiction of "Creation" on the roof of the Sistine Chapel leads the list, of course. But I never tire of "The School of Athens by" Raphael, "The Entombment" by Caravaggio, and "Saint Jerome" by Leonardo da Vinci.

Then there is the marvelous handwritten letter to the Pope from Henry VIII in which he pleads (unsuccessfully) for an annulment from his first wife, Catherine of Aragon, on the ground that she was his brother's widow.

You could easily spend weeks in that facility alone.

As a student I had earned spending money by conducting tours of the Museum, so I was able to give Lynn a better-than-average experience, -albeit somewhat hurried.

That afternoon, Lynn said she was tired, and she went back to our hotel for a nap. So I went to lunch by myself, and I ended up at one of my favorite restaurants, Tre Scalini, which has long been a fixture in Piazza Navona.

As I sat there drinking a glass of Valpolicella, I noticed a middle-aged woman sitting alone at a table near mine. She obviously spoke English, since she was reading what I once heard described, somewhat facetiously, as that "paragon of journalistic excellence," *The Rome Daily American*.

The woman looked familiar, and she was quite pretty, but I couldn't immediately put a name with her face.

For a moment I thought that she might have been an actress in one of the hundreds of Italian films I had seen over the years.

Then, all of a sudden, it dawned on me.

"No," I said out loud, "it can't be."

But it was.

I was looking at Selena Sada, my Roman tutor, and the great love of my life, who I had fallen in love with decades earlier while I was attending Bellarmine University.

The last time I had spoken to her was in 1970, shortly after I had been discharged from active duty as a Naval Officer.

I had gone to Italy to reconnect with my old friends, and most importantly with Selena.

On the day I had arrived in Rome, I had called her at her family home, and when she answered the telephone she stunned me with the news that she was home to pick up her things because she had been married that morning. She told me then that she wanted to speak with me, and she suggested that we meet at one of our old rendezvous, L'Obelisco, near Saint Peter's. But I had declined. I had told her I didn't want to interfere with her new marriage, and, very reluctantly, I had told her that I could never see her again.

But here I was, starring at her face, not ten feet away.

I eventually I got the nerve to approach her, and even though she was reading an English-language newspaper, I started in Italian.

"Selena, sono io, Jay" (Selena, it's me, Jay).

She looked up from her newspaper, obviously startled, and for a few moments she said nothing.

Then she started to cry.

I stood up and started to walk toward her, but she shook her head.

"Aspetta" (Wait), she said in Italian, "Devo pensare a cio che sta accadendo"(I have to process what is happening).

For a minute or two I stood there, feeling like an idiot.

Finally she reached out her arms and said: "Jay, vieni da me" (Jay, come to me).

So I walked over to her, put my arms around her, and hugged her silently.

After a few minutes she asked me, in English, why I was in Rome, and I told her I was on holiday with my wife.

She asked me about Lynn, and then about my life. And for more than two hours we talked about the years that had passed since our conversation on the day she was married.

It turned out, sadly, that her marriage had failed early on, and that she had remained single ever since.

But she was happy, she said, and was teaching English as a professor at Gonzaga University.

It's amazing how quickly you can pick up the pieces of an old relationship. And that was precisely what happened with Selena and me.

Of course, it didn't hurt that she was absolutely beautiful, and that she looked fifteen years younger than she actually was.

At some point she asked me if I was happy with Lynn. And of course I told her I was.

She was silent for a while, and then she returned to Italian.

"E cosi, ancora una volta, il tempismo è tutto (And so, once again, timing is everything). E ancora una volta l'accasione e persa (And once again an opportunity is lost). Ti voglio, Jay (I love you, Jay), e ti amerò fino al giorno della mia morte (and I will love you until the day I die)."

And with that we kissed and said goodbye...again. As I walked away I thought about the following lines written by William Wordsworth in his "Ode, Intimations of Immortality." Selena had committed them to memory and recited them to me as we walked in Rome's Borghese Gardens shortly before I left her and returned to the United States in 1967:

> *What though the radiance which was once so bright*
> *Be now forever taken from my sight,*
> *Though nothing can bring back the hour*
> *Of splendor in the grass, of glory in the flower;*
> *We will grieve not, rather find*
> *Strength in what remains behind;*
> *In the primal sympathy*
> *Which having been must ever be;*
> *In the soothing thoughts that spring*
> *Out of human suffering;*
> *In the faith that looks through death,*
> *In the years that bring the philosophic mind.*

Wordsworth had captured exactly the special gift that love brings to those who allow it to enter their lives, even if eventually fades or is lost.

And to conclude this part of my narrative, let me make a few observations.

If you haven't experienced love, I suggest you skip ahead to the beginning of the next chapter, and have a beer.

But if you have experienced love, let me offer these thoughts....

> ...Just as evil exists, and can be persistent, love also exists, and it, too is persistent. In fact, I believe that both evil and love transcend death.

> ...This is what is what I mean when I speak of the terms heaven and hell.

> ...When I speak of God, I am referring not to a physical person, but to the ultimate source of love.

So I can say without shame or doubt that I will love Selena, and will share in that gift that God gave me until the day I die.

That doesn't diminish my love for Lynn. She is my soul mate, and I am as devoted to her as to anything or anyone I have known in my life.

But your great love is just that.

When it comes, you should embrace it. I always will.

Chapter 32

Counting the Years

When I first passed the California Bar examination, I looked like I was about sixteen years old. In fact, one of my clients told me, jokingly (I thought), that he found it difficult to pay the hourly rate I was charging at the time to someone who looked like he was the same age as one of his children's baby-sitters.

Some people might find that amusing, or even endearing. I found it problematic.

So I did what I could to make myself look older. For example, I cut my hair quite short, at a time when most men my age had long hair.

By the time Janie graduated from grammar school, there was no danger that anyone would accuse me of looking too young. To the contrary, all of Janie's friends had parents who were considerably younger than Lynn and I, and she once complained that the problem with me was that I was "incredibly old," whatever that meant.

The truth, of course, was and is that by the time Janie was in grammar school I was a pretty old guy.

The years that had passed from the time I was a young man until the time I was nearly entitled to collect social security flew by so quickly that I couldn't tell you where they went.

The good news was that having a young child kept me motivated to stay healthy and fit. I also surrounded myself with people whose lifestyles reflected mores that were decades younger than those of my contemporaries.

When hip-hop music came on the scene I could generally tell you who was singing (or rapping), and I often knew the words.

When many of my former classmates were talking about retirement, I was expanding my horizons, and was busier than I had ever been.

I took up a new hobby, painting, that had always appealed to me, but which I shelved in favor of my law practice.

Eventually, I found myself painting whenever I had the chance, and I discovered that my new passion was both enriching and fun. Lynn helped me out, and she proved to be an exceptional teacher.

Best of all, people I had never met told me that they loved my work, and some even paid me for my paintings. This was incredibly rewarding, and gave me great satisfaction.

But my favorite pastime was simply spending time with Lynn, talking politics, philosophy, and religion, and walking along New Brighton Beach with our mangy dog, Max.

Chapter 33

Winding Down

By the time Janie was ready for high school, I was seriously contemplating retirement. I had turned down several cases that I would have taken on had I been a younger man.

Thanks to Clark Grace, a trust fund had been set up in Janie's name, and it was substantial enough to cover any school she might choose to attend.

I had hoped that school would be one of Holy Cross's public schools, all of which had excellent reputations, but Janie had different ideas. She wanted to go to Santa Monica Preparatory Academy, or SMPA, the same boarding school that her brother Joseph had attended a number of years earlier.

SMPA had been an all-male school when Joseph had gone there, but it had changed with the times, and there was now a fifty-fifty mix of girls and boys.

It still had an excellent reputation for academics, and some of Joseph's old mentors, including Father Mark Hedberg, were still teaching there.

I was reluctant to see Janie leave the nest, but on Lynn's advice, I decided to keep my mouth shut. I told her the decision was hers.

When she finally left for school, I told Lynn that I would cut back on my practice.

But before I could generate an exit strategy, I was given a case that was too good to pass up.

The case was a civil action brought by a *pro per*, Jon Strong, a retired software engineer who had sued an attorney friend of mine, Kenneth Coleman, for legal malpractice.

Strong was renowned for being a gadfly who attacked the legal system. He had sued dozens of attorneys, even judges, in what he claimed was a campaign to hold them accountable for corruption.

The gist of Strong's claim against Ken was his contention that Ken had abandoned him as a client after tapes that had been illegally recorded by Strong had been barred from use as evidence in an underlying action between Strong and a third party.

In fact, Ken had convinced the judge in the underlying action that the tapes were inadmissible, and he had done so in order to protect Strong from a sanction order. Because Ken had requested, and had been granted, the right to withdraw from Strong's defense, the notion that he had somehow abandoned Strong was absolute nonsense.

Strong wanted to use the tapes, notwithstanding their being illegal, so he accused Ken of working against him in concert with his opposing counsel.

It was all a bit nutty, but I took on the case in order to protect my friend.

What I could not predict was that this controversy would tie me up for the next five years.

It turned out that Strong was a brilliant but flawed individual who wrote well, and he generated hundreds of briefs that challenged virtually every aspect of Ken's representation of him in the underlying lawsuit.

At first, when I attended hearings on motions filed by Strong, I would refer to him as "that lunatic."

But as the years went on, I decided that insults were counter-productive, and I began treating him with the same courtesy I would extend to a fellow attorney.

To my surprise, Strong lightened up as well, and the two of us developed a relationship which was civil, if not warm or friendly.

I think it is fair to say that in a certain sense I felt sorry for this tortured soul who saw almost everyone in authority as a threat to him and his family.

Although I did everything in my power to defeat his claim against Ken, I took no great pleasure in the rulings of judge after judge who told Strong that he was abusing the legal system.

This all came to a head five years after it had started.

Strong was accused of "battering" a deputy sheriff in a courthouse in which he was asserting a civil claim against his city's mayor, and his court-appointed public defender defended the claim by asserting that Strong was mentally incompetent.

In my mind, Strong was a lot of things, including a lunatic, but he was not incompetent. In fact, when he focused on legal theories instead of on "conspiracies" against him, he was surprisingly effective.

But the judge who considered Strong's battery claim ultimately adjudged him incompetent, and that marked the end of his campaign against alleged corruption.

It is an irony in our system that "free speech" is supposed to protect lunatics as well as regular people.

Although the declaration of Strong's incompetency ultimately doomed his various civil claims, including his claim against Ken, I was – and remain – -uneasy that my victory was the product of a mental diagnosis rather than findings of fact and conclusions of law on the merits of the cases he had pursued so relentlessly.

Chapter 34

La Fine

Notwithstanding the pendency of the Strong litigation, and the time I was required to spend on that claim, my life was not the same after Janie left for boarding school.

Indeed, in the first two weeks after her departure I went through a period that was almost like mourning.

I knew she was having a wonderful experience with new friends, and that she would be just fine. But I worried about her, and I called her more often than she probably wanted, to ask if she was happy.

About a month after Janie left for SMPA, I received a telephone call from Maura.

She told me that she was flying out from Chicago, and that she and Joseph wanted to have a brief family meeting in Holy Cross with Lynn (who they now referred to as "Nana"), Janie and me.

They didn't tell me specifically what they wanted to discuss. But Maura and Joseph had both asked me how Janie was doing, and I assumed they wanted to discuss how she was assimilating into life at SMPA.

I was wrong.

When we finally got together, Joseph started the conversation by saying something that made me smile.

"Dad, we have talked it over with Nana, and we all agree that it's probably time for you to turn over your car keys."

At the time I had an old Ferrari that barely ran, and although I hadn't had any accidents, I had to admit that I was not as coordinated as I once had been.

And I was certainly losing any edge I had possessed in operating a sports car.

"I know you are right," I said, "but not being able to drive would mean that my life would change dramatically."

Lynn, who, as it turned out, was the instigator of this discussion, responded quite sensibly.

"We have discussed that, and we are all agreed that we will all help you out," she said, "and after all, I can take you anywhere you need to go."

So I handed the keys to my Ferrari key over to Joseph.

But, like my father, I had secretly kept another set of keys, and I had hidden them in the top drawer of my night table, just in case.

Credits

I would like to take this opportunity to thank some of the people who have inspired and/or helped put this book together. I apologize in advance if I haven't listed you by name.

First and foremost, Tony Seton has been a real advocate; his constant hammering on me to get down to business has been a real help.

I thank Marian and Camille for having put up with many late night and early morning sessions when I buried myself in my writing.

I also want to thank George Kriste for his help with the titles of my books, including this one, and more importantly, with daily discussions of politics, food and other interesting and thoughtful matters.

I can't overlook my walking/coffee companions, including John Wagner, "Doctor John" Harris, Rick Zug, Hudson Brett, Graeme Robertson, Dick Nystrom, Ed Barker, and Jan Durney, all of whom have given me insight into the human condition, and have helped keep me healthy as well as entertained.

Two lovely ladies, Joann Kiehn at the Pine Cone and Fiona Ayers at the Cypress Inn, have been terrific in helping me promote my books, including "signings" which have greatly benefitted a worthy charity on the Monterey Peninsula, The

Yellow Brick Road.

As my friend Denny LeVett often says, one should never overlook one's banker; so I say thanks to my friend and banker, Charles Chrietzberg, and to his wonderful family, including Sandra, Stephanie and Clark.

I also want to acknowledge several special people who support me in my life in Chicago: Mary Rose and Brendan Keleher, Patty and Paul Wohlfert, Carol Ellman and Brett Vassallo, John and Kathryn Calkins, and Patty and Bret Caldwell.

In California I have been greatly blessed by the supportive and professional staff at the Beach Club in Pebble Beach, including Debbie Monti, Tony Russo and Jason Tracy.

My discussion of politics and politicians on the Central Coast would have been impossible without the support of retired politicians Sue McCloud, Paula Hazdovac, and Karen Sharp. My actual political role was made possible by the generous contributions of hundreds of donors, including Lew Jenkins and Ron McNabb.

I don't need to mention incumbent politicians (i.e., Ken and others), because you know who you are, and besides, as Will Rogers observed, "The short memory of the American voter is what keeps our politicians in office."

Finally, and as a source of endless material and camaraderie I want to thank the Post-Tennis Bunch at the Beach Club, including (but certainly not limited to) bartender *extraordinaire* Billy Burns, and the regular (and sometimes irregular) participants in that weekly gathering: Ken Coleman, Chris Tescher, Jack Van Valkenberg, Hugh Wilson, Jack Kendall, Tom Leverone, Mark Hedberg, Michael Bowery, Gerry Maddoux, Ken Bernard, Gary Chang, Aram Kinoshian, Bobby Richards, Ron Berberian, Liam Doust, Jack Pappadeas, David Day, Rich Medel, Bill Sharpe, Jim

Heisinger, Ronnie Faia, Jody and Eric LeTowt, Jim, Ron and Zack Lowell, Randy Charles, Jonathan Sapp, Dave Sailer, Armand Kunde, Terry Russee, David Armanasco, Bill Maracco, Scot McKay and, of course, in inimitable chairman of this diverse group, Denny LeVett.

For I Have Sinned

About the Author

A native of Australia, Gerard Rose is a trial lawyer, some-time politician, and an advocate for a wide variety of noble and important civic causes. His higher education included stints at the University of Santa Clara and the Rome campus of Loyola University.

As an officer in the U.S. Navy during the 1960's, Gerard traveled throughout the western Pacific, including Vietnam. In the early 1970's he taught international law and national strategy to senior Navy officers.

Over the years he has served as scout leader; PTA president; a director of his children's grammar school; member and vice mayor of his local city council; a director of his city's redevelopment agency; president of his city's fire/ambulance authority; president of his local Gallery Alliance; and a director of his city's cultural arts center.

He is married to a clinical psychologist, and has five children and four grandchildren. He commutes on weekends between homes in California and Illinois, and while en route can usually be found reading trashy novels.

Other Books from Seton Publishing

Books by Gerard Rose

BLESS ME FATHER – His brilliant third historical novel is the extraordinary story of a man growing up during a time when a nation raises itself in a changing world.

THE BOY CAPTAIN - An historical novel about Joshua Barney, who took command of a sailing vessel in the middle of the Atlantic in the middle of a storm at age 15½.

THE EARLY TROUBLES - His first historical novel about the Irish struggle for independence during the time of the First World War.

Books by Tony Seton

THE FRANCIE LEVILLARD MYSTERIES VOLUMES ONE - FIVE - Eighteen short stories and an original play, featuring Francie LeVillard, the world's finest consulting detective.

JUST IMAGINE – A scintillating piece of fiction that tells the tale of a man returning from Heaven with a mission to tell Earthlings that they can see auras.

MAYHEM – A contemporary novel set in Marin County, California, based on the mythic struggle between good and evil, with the author being called in to tip the tide of the titanic battle.

THE AUTOBIOGRAPHY OF JOHN DOUGH, GIGOLO – A novel about a former hedge fund manager who decides on a new path – to improve the lives of women. His clients include widows, divorcees and a gangster's moll.

SILVER LINING – A novel about a shooting on the street that brings reporter David Skye and nurse Lucy Balfour together, for what becomes excitement and romance.

THE OMEGA CRYSTAL – A page-turner of a novel about how the petro industry is sitting on crucial developments in solar power, waiting until their inventories run dry.

TRUTH BE TOLD – A novelized version of a true story about an historic civil rights case of sexual harassment against a top-50 American law school.

THE QUALITY INTERVIEW / GETTING IT RIGHT ON BOTH SIDES OF THE MIC – A guide to the art of interviewing for interviewers and interviewees of every stripe.

FROM TERROR TO TRIUMPH / THE HERMA SMITH CURTIS STORY – A true story of surviving the Nazi *anchloss* of Austria to creating a successful new life on the Monterey Peninsula.

DON'T MESS WITH THE PRESS / HOW TO WRITE, PRODUCE, AND REPORT QUALITY TELEVISION NEWS - A guide to producing broadcast journalism.

RIGHT CAR, RIGHT PRICE - A simple guide that explains how to find, price, and buy the car or truck, new or used, best suited for your individual transportation needs. *Autoweek* called it "the right stuff."

If you are interested in these books, or in having your own book written, edited, and/or published, please go online to

SetonPublishing.com.

Made in the USA
Charleston, SC
16 June 2013